The Five Bells and Bladebone

"[Grimes's] best . . . as moving as it is entertaining."
—*USA Today*

"Blends almost Dickensian sketches of character and social class with glimpses of a ferocious marriage." —*Time*

"Holds the attention throughout."
—*The New York Times Book Review*

The Old Fox Deceiv'd

"A good puzzle . . . unusually well written."
—*The Boston Globe*

"Affectionately witty characterizations . . . give her writing the Dickensian touch that makes it glow."
—*The Philadelphia Inquirer*

The Man with a Load of Mischief
The first Richard Jury novel

"For readers who value wit, atmosphere, and charm in their mysteries. . . . Grimes has soaked up the atmosphere of English villages and pubs in her travels. She has learned her sleight-of-hand from Christie and delights in the rich characterizations of Marsh."
—*The Washington Post Book World*

"[Grimes's novel] is cast in the mold of the great British mysteries and comes complete with all the classic elements." —*The San Diego Union-Tribune*

ALSO BY MARTHA GRIMES

continued . . .

Martha Grimes

THE
DIRTY DUCK

A RICHARD JURY MYSTERY

AN ONYX BOOK

ONYX
Published by New American Library, a division of
Penguin Group (USA) Inc., 375 Hudson Street,
New York, New York 10014, USA
Penguin Group (Canada), 10 Alcorn Avenue, Toronto,
Ontario M4V 3B2, Canada (a division of Pearson Penguin Canada Inc.)
Penguin Books Ltd., 80 Strand, London WC2R 0RL, England
Penguin Ireland, 25 St. Stephen's Green, Dublin 2,
Ireland (a division of Penguin Books Ltd.)
Penguin Group (Australia), 250 Camberwell Road, Camberwell, Victoria 3124,
Australia (a division of Pearson Australia Group Pty. Ltd.)
Penguin Books India Pvt. Ltd., 11 Community Centre, Panchsheel Park,
New Delhi - 110 017, India
Penguin Group (NZ), cnr Airborne and Rosedale Roads, Albany,
Auckland 1310, New Zealand (a division of Pearson New Zealand Ltd.)
Penguin Books (South Africa) (Pty.) Ltd., 24 Sturdee Avenue,
Rosebank, Johannesburg 2196, South Africa

Penguin Books Ltd., Registered Offices:
80 Strand, London WC2R 0RL, England

Published by Onyx, an imprint of New American Library, a division of Penguin Group (USA) Inc. Previously published in Little, Brown and Dell editions.

First Onyx Printing, June 2004
10 9 8 7 6 5

 REGISTERED TRADEMARK—MARCA REGISTRADA

Printed in the United States of America

PUBLISHER'S NOTE
This is a work of fiction. Names, characters, places, and incidents either are the product of the author's imagination or are used fictitiously, and any resemblance to actual persons, living or dead, business establishments, events, or locales is entirely coincidental.
  The publisher does not have any control over and does not assume any responsibility for author or third-party Web sites or their content.

*To Katherine,
and J. Mezzanine*

*and in memory of George Roland
1930–83*

I

STRATFORD

" 'Whoever loved that loved not at first sight?' "

—As You Like It

1

The doors of the Royal Shakespeare Theatre emptied another audience into a mean rain that always seemed to know the minute the performance ended. Tonight's play had been *As You Like It*, and the faces of the crowd wore that disoriented look that said they hadn't quite got their bearings, as if by some magical permutation the bucolic airiness of the Forest of Arden still glittered out here in the dark and the drizzle.

The crowd fanned out down walks and winding streets and disappeared into parked cars and pubs. The lights around the theatre went out, cutting bright coins from the river, as if a stagehand had thrown a switch in the water.

The Black Swan—or the Dirty Duck, depending upon the prospective patron's approach— was strategically placed across the street from the side of the theatre. Its double-sided sign (flying swan on one side, drunken duck on the other) sometimes resulted in missed rendezvous for strangers to the town who agreed to meet at one and then came upon the other.

Five minutes after the curtain came down, the Dirty Duck was chock-a-block with people getting as drunk as possible before Time was called. The crowd in the room inside overflowed onto the walled terrace outside. Smoke from cigarettes hazed the night like one of London's old yellow fogs. It was summer and the tourist season was in full swing; most of the accents were American.

One of these Americans, Miss Gwendolyn Bracegirdle, who had never had more than an ounce of sweet sherry at a time on the veranda of her huge pink-stuccoed house in Sarasota, Florida, was standing with a friend in a shadowy corner of the terrace getting sloshed.

"Oh, *honey*, not *another!* This here's my second—what do they call it?"

"Gin." Her companion laughed.

"Gin!" She giggled. "I definitely *couldn't!*" But she held her glass in a way that said she definitely could.

"Just pretend it's a very dry martini."

Miss Bracegirdle giggled again as her glass was taken from her for a refill. From sweet sherry to martinis was a giant step for Gwendolyn Bracegirdle, if not for all mankind.

Smiling vaguely, she looked around the terrace at the other patrons, but no one smiled back. Gwendolyn Bracegirdle was not the type who would engrave herself on the memories of others, as others did on her memory. (As she had been telling her friend—if there was one thing she knew, it was faces.) Gwendolyn herself was unmemorable—short, pudgy, and permed; the only thing that set her apart tonight was that she was overdressed in beaded brocade. Her glance fell on an elderly angular woman whose damp and lugubrious eye made her think of her mother. She sobered up a little; Mama Bracegirdle did not hold with spiritous liquors, at least none but the ones she herself took for medicinal purposes. Mama had a whole raft of ailments. Right now (given the five-hour time difference) she was probably fanning herself on the porch of the Pink Horror; at least Gwendolyn, now three thousand miles away, and used to daub and wattle and thatch, thought of it as a Pink Horror.

As another cold drink was put into her hand, and her friend smiled at her, Gwendolyn said, "I just don't know how on *earth* I'll ever find my way back to my room again." A dreary enough room it was, too: top-floor rear with a lumpy bed and a hot-and-cold basin. Bath all the way down the hall. She could have afforded much better, but she had chosen the Diamond Hill Guest House because it seemed so awfully English-y, staying at a Bed-and-Breakfast. Not being catered to like the others on her tour who were living in Americanized luxury at the Hilton and other expensive hotels. Gwendolyn believed firmly in the when-in-Rome theory, not lying back in the Hilton and calling room service just like you did in the States.

"I don't know how I'll get there on my own," she said again, smiling coyly.

"I'll see you get home."

The young girl behind the bar of the Dirty Duck was calling Time.

"Let's have one last one before we leave."

"*Another?* But I'm hardly into *this*—well, if you *insist* . . ."

During her friend's absence she gave herself a quick once-over in her pocket mirror, running her little finger around the outline of her Passion Flower lipstick. Seeing the pale lips and rouge-less faces of many of the women around her, looking almost ghostly in the hazy darkness, she thought perhaps she had overdone the color.

"Whoo-*ee*," said Gwendolyn, fanning herself with her hand as the fourth gin appeared in front of her. "These pubs get so *crowded*. I swear, it's hotter'n back in Sarasota. There's so many British are going over there these days. But they go to Miami, I guess, when it's really the West Coast that's nicest. . . . Listen, wasn't that play wonderful? Wouldn't it be just *wonderful* to have nothing to do all day but live in the Forest of Arden? I can't understand why what's-his-name was so *melancholy*—"

"Jacques, you mean."

"Um. He reminds me of someone I know back in Sarasota. The actor, I mean. Like I told you, Mama always did say, 'Gwennie, it's absolutely *uncanny* how you can know faces.' Mama always said I can read faces like the blind." Actually, Mama had never said any such thing; Mama never told her anything nice about herself. Probably why she had this sort of . . . complex. Gwendolyn could feel her face burning, and she quickly changed the subject. "It's too bad I didn't see you before the play started. There was an empty seat next to mine up until intermission when some kid grabbed it. Could you see all right up there in the balcony?" Her companion nodded as the barmaid called Time again. Gwendolyn sighed. "I think it's too bad the pubs have to close up so early the way they do. I mean you're just getting all convivial and you have to stop. . . . Wouldn't it be nice if we could only go for a drive?" That made Gwendolyn think of the old Caddy Mama kept garaged all the time, only taking it out for weddings and funerals. Gwendolyn called it The Iron Maiden. The Caddy even reminded her of Mama, the way she was always dressed in hard-looking gray or black with a metallic sheen to the material, her gray eyes flecked with tiny bands like wheel spokes, her gray hair pulled back in a hubcap bun. Just like that old car.

"Well, we could go for a walk before you go home. I like to walk by the river."

"Why, that *would* be nice," said Gwendolyn. She emptied her glass, nearly choking on the harsh taste of the gin Mama considered a ticket to hell, and gathered up her beaded purse. She felt overdressed in the blue brocade. But if you couldn't dress to go to the Royal Shakespeare Theatre, when could you? Some of these people, she thought as the two of them walked out, would wear jeans to a Coronation.

The Dirty Duck emptied in that near-magical way that pubs do. When they close, they close; it's as if suddenly the publican had grown five extra hands with which to whisk glasses from tables; and on the drinker's end of it, as if that last swallow, that final drop were the only thing keeping him from the dark Angel.

As the two of them crossed the road, the lights were already dimming in the Dirty Duck. They took the unlit path that curved around the brass-rubbing center and walked on toward the church—a leisurely walk in which they chatted about the play.

When they had circled round behind the Church of the Holy Trinity, her friend paused. "Why're we stopping?" asked Gwendolyn, hoping she knew. She tried to suppress the excitement building inside her, but it rose up much like the hatred had risen thinking of Mama. The dusty passion was something she didn't understand and was intensely ashamed of. But after all (she told herself), there was nothing wrong *these* days with *who* you got those feelings about. And the shame was part of the excitement, she knew. Her face burned. Well, it was all Mama's fault. If she hadn't kept Gwendolyn garaged up along with the Caddy all these years . . .

Her friend's voice broke into her reflections, with a little laugh. "Sorry, but it must be all of those drinks. There are toilets over there. . . ."

They walked over to the whitewashed, tiny building, much used by tourists during the day, but as black as the path they had walked along at night. The excitement was building inside Gwendolyn all the while.

"I hope you don't mind."

Gwendolyn giggled. "Well, of course not. Only, look. There's a sign says Out of Order—"

About as far as Gwendolyn Bracegirdle had ever got toward experiencing what Shakespeare called the act of darkness was when she'd had to remove the hand of a gentleman friend from her knee. She had realized long ago that she was painfully lacking in sex appeal.

Thus it was to her credit that when she felt herself gently pushed inside the public toilets, and felt hands on her shoulders, felt breath on her neck, and felt, finally, this looseness, as if brocade, bra, slip had suddenly fallen away—it was to her credit that instead of fighting off this affront to her person, she said to herself, *The hell with it, Mama! I'm about to be ravished!*

And when she felt that funny, tickling sensation somewhere around her breast, she almost giggled, thinking, *The silly fool's got a feather* . . .

The silly fool had a razor.

2

Willow-laced and sheeted with light, the River Avon flowed from the rose-hued brick theatre to the Church of the Holy Trinity. Ducks slept in the rushes; swans drifted dreamlike along its banks.

One would not have been surprised on such a morning, in such a place, to see Rosalind reading poems tacked to trees, or Jacques brooding beside the riverbank.

Indeed, from a distance, one might have mistaken the lady and gentleman by the river between the old church and the theatre as two characters who had wandered out of a Shakespearean play to this sylvan river to feed the swans.

It was an Arcadian idyll, a reverie, a dream . . .

Almost.

"You've fed my last fairy cake to the swans, Melrose," said the lady who was not Rosalind, poking her face into a white paper bag.

"It was stale," said the gentleman who, although melancholy, was not Jacques. Melrose Plant wondered if the Avon at this point was deep enough to drown in. But why bother? In another five minutes he'd be bored to death, anyway.

"I was saving them for my elevenses," said Lady Agatha Ardry, grumpily.

Melrose looked out over the silver waters of the Avon and sighed. What a pastoral scene it was, fit for a shepherdess or a milkmaid. A shepherdess with violet eyes would suit him to perfection. His thoughts drifted like the crumbs on the water back to Littlebourne and Polly Praed. But he could not imagine Polly carrying a pail of milk.

"We're all having morning coffee at the Cobweb Tea Room. Surely, you'll come down off your high horse and join us," she said, reproachfully.

"No. I thought I'd have my elevenses up on my high horse."

"You really do put yourself forward, Plant, in the most annoying fashion—"

"Putting myself forward is precisely what I'm *not* doing. To wit, I am not having morning coffee at the Cobweb Tea Room."

"You've not even met them yet."

"That's right."

They were her cousins from Milwaukee, Wisconsin. Thus far, Melrose had seen them only from a distance. He would go no nearer, no matter how she exhorted him. He had made his own accommodation at the Falstaff Hotel, a very small but charming place on the main street, thus forcing Agatha and the American cousins into other, more touristy quarters. He had seen them on the walk in front of the Hathaway's heavy-handed mock-Tudor, swarming all over the pavement: cousins, second cousins, cousins several-times-removed—a veritable flotilla of cousins had come here on one of those tour buses. Two weeks ago at Ardry End she had waved the letter in his face and insisted that he really *must* meet them. "Our American cousins, the Randolph Biggets."

"Not mine, I assure you," Melrose had replied from behind his morning paper.

"By marriage, my dear Plant," Agatha said with a self-satisfied look, as if she'd got him there.

"Not by my marriage. That was my uncle Robert's responsibility, and he has passed on."

"Do stop being difficult, Plant."

"I am not being difficult. I did not marry the Randolph Biggets."

"You don't want to meet your own *kin*?"

"Less than kin and less than kind, to paraphrase Hamlet. Hamlet would have been ever so much happier had he hewn to that rule. But I suppose if Claudius had been named Randolph Bigget, Hamlet might not have had so much trouble killing him whilst he prayed."

As Agatha counted over the various offerings on the tea trolley, she said smugly, "Well, then, the mountain will have to come to Mahomet."

Melrose put down his paper. That sounded ominous. "What do you mean?"

Derobing a pink-frosted fairy cake, she said, "Only that if we can't go *there*, I shall just have to ask the Biggets to come *here*. Yes, a visit to the countryside . . . yes, I expect they would like that."

Here? Melrose knew blackmail when he heard it. But he feigned ignorance by saying, "You've only the two rooms in your cottage. I expect, though, that you could put them up at the Jack and Hammer. Dick Scroggs always has the spare room. Especially since that murder three years ago." He filled in a few more blanks in his crossword puzzle.

"You really do have the *most* morbid sense of humor, Plant. And with all of these rooms at Ardry End, I should certainly think you could be a bit more hospitable." When he did not reply, she added, "Then if you won't offer them a bed, you must have them round for one of Martha's cream teas."

"They shouldn't be having cream teas. I'm sure they're quite stout enough." Melrose entered *oaf* in the down line beginning with *L*.

"Stout? You've never even seen them."

"They sound stout."

Wild horses could not have dragged Melrose

to Stratford-upon-Avon in the month of July. But the call from Richard Jury two days before could. Since it was not all that far from Long Piddleton, and since Jury would be there on some sort of routine police business, he had suggested that Plant, if he had no more pressing commitments, motor along.

And motor along he had, Agatha doing the driving from the passenger's seat, with a cold collation in a wicker basket held firmly on her lap.

"Dear old Stratford," said Agatha now, arms outspread as if she meant to take the town to her bosom.

Melrose watched her cross the street, heading for the Cobweb, where she was to meet her cousins for morning coffee in the darkness of sturdy beams and tilting floors. The less light, the wobblier the tiny tables, the more the tourists approved. Agatha certainly did, though the state of the table was less important to her than the state of the cake plate. Had she known he was supposed to meet Richard Jury for dinner, Melrose would never have been rid of her.

For not only would she be missing out on Jury, she would be missing out on a free meal.

Stratford's Church of the Holy Trinity lay at the end of an avenue of limes. William Shakespeare was buried there, and Melrose wanted to see its chancel. The heavy door closed softly behind him, as if more conscious of genius than of the knot of pilgrims at the souvenir counter buying up anything stamped with the playwright's image—bookmarks, keyrings, address books. No one was visible in the church proper, other than an elderly man at a collection box stationed at the foot of the nave. Melrose fished out the ten pence it would cost him to have a look at Shakespeare's resting place. Rather like being admitted to a ride in an amusement park, he thought. It made him feel a bit ghoulish: apparently, the guardian of the grave was not of the same mind, for he smiled broadly at Melrose and lifted the red velvet rope.

William Shakespeare must have been a man of taste. If there were ever anyone more deserving of a full-length effigy in marble, a little dog at his feet, sarcophagus set back in its own velvet-draped chapel—surely it was Shakespeare. Instead, there was only this small bronze plaque bearing his name, one name among others in his family, buried beside him. Melrose felt an uncustomary surge of near-religious respect for such genius, so lacking in ostentation.

Before he left the nave, Melrose examined the choir and the unusual carvings of small gargoyle-like faces on the arms of the seats. As he took a step backward he found his leg had struck something, which turned out to be the hindquarters of someone stooping down between the tiered benches.

"Oh, sorry," said the youngish man, scrambling to his feet and adjusting a strap over his shoulder, which was attached to a rather large square case. At first Melrose thought it must be some elaborate camera equipment, except that the case was metal. A Geiger counter, perhaps? Was the chap looking for some radioactive material in the choir? "Did you lose something?" Melrose asked, politely.

"Oh, no. Just looking underneath the seats." The wooden benches folded up against the backs when not in use. Not all of them had been returned to their upright position. "At the carvings. They've even got them underneath," he explained.

"The misericords, you mean?"

"That what they're called? Funny things. Whyever'd anyone carve them there?"

"I don't know."

Melrose decided that he was somewhere in his late thirties, not quite so young as he'd supposed; it was that fresh-faced look, as if he'd been scrubbed by a hard-bristled brush, that was deceptive. He was fairly tall, brown-haired, and undistinguished-looking in his seersucker suit and perfectly hideous polka-dotted bow tie. He ran his finger around his collar in the manner of a man who disliked ties. His accent was either American or Canadian; Melrose had never tuned his ear to the difference. Most likely American.

"You from around here?" the man asked, as he followed Melrose up the nave and past the guardian of the red velvet cord.

"No, just visiting."

"Yeah, me too." His tone suggested that he had finally found a comrade in this vast wasteland of Stratford, as if all of the visitors here were wandering in the desert. "Neat church, isn't it?"

"Neat, yes."

The American stopped among the chairs and prayer cushions and shot out a blunt, spatulate-fingered hand. "Harvey L. Schoenberg from D.C."

"I'm Melrose Plant." He shook the other man's hand.

"Where from?"

"Northants. That is, Northamptonshire. It's about sixty or seventy miles from here."

"Never been there."

"Most visitors haven't. Nothing there especially interesting except rather pretty villages in rather pretty country."

"Listen," said Harvey Schoenberg, shouldering open the heavy door of the church, "don't knock it." He said it as if Melrose had been discrediting his homeland. "I only wish July was like this in D.C."

"Exactly where is Deezey?" asked Melrose, puzzled.

Schoenberg laughed. "*You* know. Washington, D.C."

"Ah. Your capital city."

"Yeah. Of the good old U.S. of A. Hell of a climate, though, let me tell you."

Melrose had just decided to leave the church walk for the riverbank when Schoenberg, walking beside him, said, "Who's Lucy?"

"What?"

"Lucy." Schoenberg pointed down at the stone walk. The inscription lay carved in the stone at their feet. "She a friend of Shakespeare's or something?"

"I think it's probably a family name, the Lucys." With his silver-knobbed walking stick, Melrose pointed to the left and right, to the ground beneath the lime trees. "Buried there or here, I imagine."

"Weird. We walking on graves?"

"Um. Well, I thought I'd walk by the river, Mr. Schoenberg. Nice meeting—"

"Okay." He hitched the strap of the big metal box farther up on his shoulder and continued with Melrose across the grass. He was rather like a lost dog whose head one had patted in the park and who wasn't about to let one off so easily.

"I notice things," said Schoenberg, folding a

stick of gum into his mouth, "because I'm collecting information for a book."

It would, Melrose thought, be ungentlemanly of him not to inquire into its nature, and so he did.

"It's on Shakespeare," said Schoenberg, chomping away happily.

Inwardly, Melrose heaved a sigh. Oh, dear. Why in heaven's name would this American, his face as freshly scrubbed as a new potato, want to go wading into the shoals of *those* dangerous waters?

"There must be a whole sea of books on Shakespeare, Mr. Schoenberg; aren't you afraid you'll drown?"

"Harve. Drown? Hell, no. What I've got is something completely new. It's really more on Kit Marlowe than Shakespeare."

Melrose was almost afraid to ask: "Exactly what is your subject? I hope it hasn't to do with establishing authenticity."

"Authenticity? Meaning who wrote them?" Schoenberg shook his head. "I'm writing about life more than literature. It's really Marlowe I'm interested in, anyway."

"I see. As a scholar? Are you affiliated with some institution?"

"Never even got my master's. I leave the egghead crap to my brother. He's chairman of English at this college in Virginia. I'm meeting him in London in a few days. Me, I'm a com-

THE DIRTY DUCK   *21*

puter programmer." He patted the metal box
and hitched the strap up on his shoulder.

"Really? I have always felt there were far too
many department chairmen in the world and far
too few computer programmers."

Harvey Schoenberg's smile was wide. "Well,
there's going to be a lot more, Mel. The computer is going to change the world. Like this little baby, here." And he tapped the box as if it
were a bundle of literal baby.

Melrose stopped in his tracks, and some hungry swans, hoping for action, rowed over. "You
don't mean to tell me, Mr. Schoenberg—"

"Harve."

"—that *that* is a *computer?*"

Harvey Schoenberg's dark eyes glittered
through the cobweb of shadows the willows cast
across his face. "You bet your little booties, Mel.
Want to see it? On second thought, let me buy
you a beer and I'll tell you all about it. Okay?"

Not staying for an answer, Harvey started
walking away.

"Well, I—" Melrose was not sure he wanted to
know all about it.

"Come on, come on," motioned Harvey
Schoenberg, as if they were about to miss a bus.
"The Dirty Duck's just across the street. Or the
Black Swan, whichever. How come it's got two
names?"

"The Black Swan section is their restaurant, I
believe."

Schoenberg looked over his shoulder at the river. "Where do they get the swans? Just for fun I checked them out and ran a little program on them to see which time of day was the least likely for them to crowd up at the bank for crumbs. The Ishi figured it all out for me."

Melrose was not quite sure from which end to approach this information. "I suppose they get the swans from a swannery."

"No kidding. Kind of like a chicken farm, or something?"

The Black Swan was just ahead. Melrose felt the need of a drink. "Not exactly." He gazed up at the bright blue sky and wondered if he had a touch of sun-madness. "What," he asked, "is an Ishi?"

"Ishikabi. This little baby. Japanese, converted by yours very truly."

Harvey Schoenberg was clearly on a nick-name basis with everything in the world, including his computer.

Sun-madness relieved by a drink of Old Pe-culier, Melrose waited—not without trepida-tion—for Harvey Schoenberg to sort it all out. The Ishi sat on a chair near Harvey, making a third at their party. The front of the case had been lifted to display a small screen and a key-board. There were a couple of slots for some disks, and on the green screen pulsed a tiny white square. The Ishi's heartbeat, apparently. It throbbed so rapidly there that Melrose was sure it and Harvey were both raring to go.

"*Who Killed Marlowe?*" said Harvey Schoenberg.

"Well, no one is quite certain what hap—"

But Harvey was shaking his head so hard his bow tie bobbed, and he adjusted it. "No, no. That's the name of my book: *Who Killed Marlowe?*"

"Really?" Melrose cleared his throat.

"Now,"—Harvey leaned over his folded arms across the small table so that his nose was not all that far from Melrose's own—"tell me what you know about Kit Marlowe."

Melrose thought for a moment. "Kit, that is, Christopher,"—Melrose hadn't quite Harvey's genius for nestling up to strangers—"Marlowe died in a tavern brawl, as I remember, drinking in a pub in Southwark—"

"Deptford."

"Ah, yes, Deptford—when there was some sort of disagreement and Marlowe was stabbed by accident. Well, something like that," ended Melrose, seeing a sort of piratical smile on Schoenberg's face.

"Go on."

Melrose shrugged. "With what? That's all I know."

"I mean about the rest of his life. The plays and so forth."

"I was under the impression you weren't interested in the literary aspect."

"I'm not, not like the eggheads who keep fooling around with the bard's stuff, trying to show that guys like Bacon wrote Shakespeare. But Marlowe's relationship with Shakespeare, now *that's* something else."

"I don't think Christopher Marlowe and Shakespeare were all that friendly. Marlowe's reputation was pretty well established when Shakespeare came along. He'd already got *Tamburlaine* and *Doctor Faustus* on the boards and was thought to be perhaps the best playwright in England. Then there was something about his politics. Marlowe was an agent, a sort of spy . . ."

As Melrose's recitation continued, Harvey sat there nodding away energetically, like the teacher waiting for the idiot-student to complete his rote-learning so the tutor could jump in and correct it.

"*Tamburlaine* was written while Marlowe was still a student at Cambridge, or at least part of it was. Amazing piece of writing for someone that young. Then there was *Doctor Faustus*—"

" 'Was this the face that launched a thousand ships,' " said Harvey, rather sadly.

"That's right." Melrose warmed to him a little. "How'm I doing?"

"Great. You really know a lot. You a professor, or something?"

"I do occasionally turn my hand at lecturing at one of the universities. Nothing much." Melrose drained his glass of beer and poured the remaining dregs from the Old Peculier—which was strong stuff—or from Harvey Schoenberg—even stronger stuff—he didn't know.

"Literature, right?"

"French poetry. But getting back to Marlowe—"

Leaning closer, his voice low and level, Harvey said: "The Earl of Southampton. What do you know about him?"

Had Melrose been standing in a rained-on doorway with his coat collar turned up he couldn't have felt more like he was passing along secret information. "Southampton? Wasn't he Shakespeare's patron? A patron of the arts?"

"Correct. Young, rich, handsome. Pretty boy Southampton."

"Really, now. You're not suggesting Shakespeare's sexual life was suspect. I think that's rot."

Harvey seemed surprised. "You read the sonnets?"

"Yes. That doesn't show anything but affection, loyalty—"

"You could've fooled me." He leaned over the Ishi computer and did some of the fastest fingerwork Melrose had ever seen. The tiny white square jumped around and words scrolled up the screen.

> *Bound for the prize of all too precious you,*
> *That did my ripe thoughts in my brain*
>   *inhearse—*

He seemed to think this was indisputable evidence. "If the shoe fits . . . But that's not the point. Hell, I don't care what these guys did in bed. Of course, we all know Marlowe was a little Nellie—"

"We do?"

"Sure. What the hell do you think all that Walsingham business was about? Oh, I know *one* of the theories says that Kit got stabbed in a brawl over some dame of 'ill-repute' and died from it. Then there was some other big deal about Marlowe whooping it up on a pleasure-boat and getting in a fight and going overboard." Harvey snorted, thereby sending both theories to their watery grave. "Listen, don't you believe it. It was Tom Walsingham who was Marlowe's real *friend*." Harvey winked and adjusted the awful bow-tie. "*Hero and Leander*'s dedicated to him." Harvey shoved his glass aside and leaned toward Melrose as if the two of them were running spies. "The Walsingham family had plenty of dough and plenty of influence. It was Tommy-boy that recruited Kit as a mole—"

Melrose cleared his throat. "What century are we in, Mr. Schoenberg?"

"Harve—and got him sent off to Spain and planted in an abbey to find out what the Catholics were up to. You know. Mary, Queen of Scots. That bunch." Harvey sat back, drank his beer.

"I've heard of her, yes."

Harvey sat forward. "*Well?* No wonder Kit nearly wigged out when they tossed him in the slammer. Tom Walsingham had influence, for God's sakes. He could have prevented all that. So what's he do? Lets Kit take the rap . . ." Harvey waved his hand in disgust. "Like the CIA or M-5. 'But if you're caught, Double-O-Seven, we don't know you,' et cetera."

In spite of himself, Melrose persisted: "We're talking about a time of extraordinary political and religious conflict. You couldn't go round espousing the seemingly heretical ideas of a Faustus and in your personal life go round spying on the Catholics in Spain without getting into trouble—"

Harvey Schoenberg made a dismissive gesture. "Big deal. And on top of that there was the plague. Bad news, a plague." Harvey inspected his nails as if looking for telling signs. "I know all of that. But, see, that's where everybody got off on the wrong foot about Marlowe's death. The ones who don't think he was killed by accident—*accident!*—you ever hear of someone getting a sword in his eye by accident?" Harvey shook his head at the sort of scholarship which could attempt to birth a lion and bring forth a gnat. "So that's out. Where the mistake was, was that the ones who knew Kit was murdered thought those guys who met him in the tavern in Deptford killed him for political reasons; that they were afraid if Kit was taken in he'd spill his guts about Walsingham and Raleigh and the whole schmeer."

Melrose had been picking the label from his bottle of beer throughout this discourse, an unpleasant habit which he had, up until now, never stooped to. "I take it you think otherwise?"

Once again, Harvey leaned toward him and lowered his voice. "Listen, for four hundred years people have been trying to prove what happened in that tavern in Deptford. The only witnesses, too bad, were the principals, right?— there was this Poley, Skeres, Frizer. And Marlowe, but he was dead, poor bastard—"

"One of the greatest, if not *the* greatest loss to English literature we've ever known." Melrose, who seldom pontificated, felt a need to. Actually, he felt rather drunk. A defense, no doubt, against the hounds of total unreason. "Twenty-nine, he was—"

Literary loss cut no ice with Harvey Schoenberg. He had bigger fish to fry. "Yeah, he died. But that's life. The point is, most people seem to think this Skeres and Frizer were like hit men for Walsingham and it was, like I said, political. Well, you know what I say to that?"

"I can't imagine."

"Bullshit." Schoenberg sat back, looking smug, arm draped over back of chair.

"Really?" Melrose was almost afraid to ask, but felt his resistance had been pretty much worn down to the ground. "What happened, then? Who do you think was responsible?"

Harvey Schoenberg flashed that smile at him, piratical, conspiratorial, like a man with a knife between his teeth. "You won't tell anyone my theory?" And again he tapped the computer. "I got it all in here, all the evidence."

"Tell anyone? I guarantee they could put me on the rack and I wouldn't breathe a word of it."

"Shakespeare," said Harvey Schoenberg, happily drinking off the dregs of his pint.

3

Melrose stared at him. But Harvey Schoenberg seemed not at all distraught that he had just come to the most imbecilic conclusion in literary history.

"Are you really trying to tell me that you think William Shakespeare was responsible for the death of Christopher Marlowe?"

Harvey's gray eyes glittered like shards from a broken mirror. He smiled. He nodded. He offered Melrose a cigarette from a pack of Salems.

"You're talking about the greatest writer who ever lived."

"What's that got to do with the price of eggs?" Harvey leaned across and lit Melrose's cigarette. "I mean, temperamentally speaking, you know what writers and painters and so forth are like. Unstable. Geniuses are probably the nuttiest of all."

"Shakespeare was *not* 'nutty.'" Melrose coughed on the smoke of the minty-tasting cigarette. "Indeed, from what we know of him, Shakespeare was an extremely sensible, level-headed businessman." Why was he arguing with this American and his crazy theories? The legacy of too many talks with Agatha, perhaps?

Harvey hitched one foot up on his chair, leaned his chin on his knee. "Point is, what do we *really* know about any of these guys back then? Hell, they didn't even spell their own *names* the same way twice." He dribbled ash on the floor. "Marloe, Marley, Marlowe, even Marlin—I must've counted seven, eight different spellings—how the hell can we tell what they signed or wrote or what?"

"For what motive? What earthly motive would Shakespeare have for doing away with Marlowe?"

Harvey leaned back over the table and said, "Mel, haven't you been listening? The Earl of Southampton, that's why."

"But the Earl of Southampton was *Shakespeare*'s patron! Not Marlowe's. That wouldn't—"

Harvey sighed, as if he were tired of repeating a lesson that should have been learned long ago. Once again, he turned to the computer, punched the keys and said, "If you don't think there was enough jealousy going there to sink a battleship, then you're nuts. You said you read the sonnets. Well, just look at this."

Whilst I alone did call upon thy aid,
My verse alone had all thy gentle grace;
But now my gracious numbers are decay'd,

And my sick Muse doth give another place.
I grant, sweet love, thy lovely argument
Deserves the travail of a worthier pen;
Yet what of thee thy poet doth invent
He robs thee of, and pays it thee again.
He lends thee virtue, and he stole that word
From thy behaviour; beauty doth he give,
And found it in thy cheek: he can afford
No praise to thee but what in thee doth live.
  Then thank him not for that which he doth say,
  Since what he owes thee thou thyself dost pay.

"Can you feature it? 'Give another place, 'et cetera. Look at that language and don't tell me Shakespeare couldn't have stuck a dagger in Marlowe's eye. Though I'm not saying, of course, Shakespeare did his own dirty work. He sent Nick Skeres and Frizer—"

"They were *Walsingham*'s men, for God's sakes, not Shakespeare's!"

"Well, Billy-boy knew them; I mean all of these guys knew each other."

"What proof do you have—?"

But Harvey was too busy punching keys and running the little white square around to pay attention to Melrose's weak-kneed questions. "That last poem doesn't cut ice with you, just look at this one again."

Bound for the prize of all too precious you,
That did my ripe thoughts in my brain inhearse,

Making their tomb the womb wherein they grew?
Was it his spirit, by spirits taught to write
Above a mortal pitch, that struck me dead?

"What do you think of that? Look at that 'struck me dead.' To tell the truth I wouldn't be a bit surprised Will Shakespeare didn't want to get to Kit Marlowe before Kit got to him. Wonder what *inhearse* means," he added, idly.

Now the man apparently was entertaining the idea that Christopher Marlowe was murdered because Shakespeare was afraid Marlowe might murder Shakespeare. Melrose felt he ought to fight a duel or something. Just lay his glove across Schoenberg's face and give him choice of weapons.

"And then there's that sonnet that looks like a suicide threat—want me to scroll up to that—?"

"No thank you. Please don't scroll anywhere. I find that I am late to an important appointment—"

"Gee, not even time for another drink?"

"Not unless it's hemlock, Mr. Schoenberg." Remembering he was a gentleman, Melrose forced a wintry smile.

"Harve. Hey, that's rich. I really got you going, didn't I? . . . Well, it doesn't surprise me. I mean, the world probably isn't ready for heavy stuff like this. But, believe me, I got all the evidence in this little beauty." He patted the Ishikabi computer. As Melrose gathered up his walking stick, Harvey Schoenberg said, "You going to see *Hamlet?*"

Melrose was almost afraid to answer. "I expect so." He and Jury had tickets in the stalls.

"Man, I wouldn't miss it. There's all sorts of evidence . . . it's a revenge tragedy, you know."

"Really?"

"They're all the same. Now Kyd—Tom Kyd, I mean—was a good friend of Marlowe's; but all I can say is, with friends like that—who needs enemies?" Schoenberg waved him back. "Come on, sit down a minute, I want to show you something."

With a sort of dreadful fascination, as if he had been hypnotized by the snake's eye of the computer, Melrose sat down again.

Harvey punched the keys around, saying, "Can you feature it? Kyd saying all this stuff against Marlowe?"

"*. . . amongst those waste and idle papers (which I carde not for) & which vnaskt I did deliuer vp, were founde some fragmentes of a disputation toching that opinion affirmed by Marlowe to be his, and shufled with some of myne (unknown to me) by some occasion of our wrythinge in one chamber twoe yeares synce. . . . That I shold loue or be familer frend, with one so irreligious, were verie rare . . . he was intemperate & of a cruel hart . . . an athiest . . .*"

"Of course, we have to remember Kyd was being tortured into giving evidence against Marlowe—"

Melrose, quite familiar by now with torture, rose. "It's been most enlightening, Mr. Schoenberg."

"Harve. Kyd wrote *The Spanish Tragedy*—"

"I know," said Melrose icily.

Harvey Schoenberg sighed. "Like I said, read one, you've read 'em all. Those revenge tragedies are all alike."

Melrose had to argue, despite himself. "I would certainly not class *Hamlet* in the general category of revenge—"

He was not to be permitted to complete his thought, apparently.

"Why? Same old stuff. Trouble is, Hamlet wanted revenge on Claudius and went around killing all the wrong people before he finally got around to the right one."

Melrose had to admit it was a refreshingly simple way to look at *Hamlet*.

4

Detective Superintendent Richard Jury was not kidding himself.

He knew that stopping here to visit his old friend Sam Lasko had merely been an excuse to spend a few days in Stratford, so that he could appear, as if by some strange coincidence, on Jenny Kennington's doorstep.

He sat with his feet up on Detective Sergeant Lasko's cluttered desk, scanning the Stratford telephone directory. He was trying to look awfully casual about the search for the number; he was certain the lady in the corner—Lasko's secretary—had eyes like lasers beneath those heavy brows and hornrimmed glasses with which she could burn straight through the telephone book to the page of *K*'s he was scouring, and then smile meanly and go tell the world. Jury tried to empty his mind. Probably, she was a mindreader too.

He found the entry *Kennington, J.*, and picked up a pencil and wrote it into his notebook. And then, telling himself he was really only looking for the best route to London, he got up and looked at the blow-up of a map of Stratford. She lived in the old part of Stratford—

"Can I help you find something, Superintendent?"

The voice hit him between the shoulder blades. Quickly, he turned. Was she laughing, secretly? "What? No. No, I was just looking up the route to London."

"What's the matter," she asked, "with the one you came on?" She *zapped* her page from the typewriter, and smiled her psychic's smile.

He started to mumble something about construction and road workers but decided she would find out later that he was lying, so he said nothing. But she was rolling another sheet into the typewriter, as if the question had been an idle one anyway.

Sap, he thought, not of her but of himself. Jury leaned back in Lasko's chair, and wondered what it was in his nature that kept him impervious to the siren song of some truly seductive women, but made him take a dive for another sort—

All of this water imagery was transporting him to the banks of the Avon, where his imagination rid Stratford of all its tourists and replaced them with Jenny, walking there alone. The iridescent blues and greens of the ducks bobbed sleepily in the reeds and rushes; the swans slid by in the cool, companionable stream. His mind snapped pictures: ducks, swans, Jenny Kennington. Then it moved forward to September. September would be even better. Sunlight filtering through the trees, a skin of golden light on the water. October. Better yet. Cold enough that she would start rubbing her arms and need someone to warm her up. . . .

Ducks bobbed and swans floated up there behind the scrim of the station ceiling and Jury thought of a way to put all of this magic-act into operation. Why not invite her to dinner with him and Melrose Plant at the Black Swan tonight? And the theatre afterward? For her, safety in numbers. Plant wouldn't mind, certainly, although he hadn't met her when he'd been in Littlebourne last year—

Hold it, mate. Melrose Plant must be one of the most eligible men in the whole of the British Isles. He had intelligence, looks, character, warmth. Whether Jury had enough of those himself, he didn't know. But he knew damned well he didn't have the rest of it, like money. Melrose Plant was filthy rich. And titles. Though Plant had given them up, his titles trailed after him like the wake of a ship. The Earl of Caverness. Lord Ardry. Twelfth Viscount in the Ardry-Plant line—

Lady Kennington and Lord Ardry . . .

Forget dinner at the Black Swan.

This is ridiculous! You're a policeman! He surged out of Lasko's chair.

"*I* am?"

To Jury's everlasting mortification he found he had spoken aloud. He was saved from replying by the blessed and sudden appearance of Detective Sergeant Lasko, who at that moment came through the door.

"Trouble over at the Hilton," he said, tossing a cap which failed to meet with an old coatrack. Lasko had a basset-hound sort of face, eyes and folds of skin beneath them pulled down by weights of sadness. His temperament matched his looks. He moved slowly, as if constricted by his blanket of gloom.

"Trouble?" asked Jury, happy for anything which would pull the typist's eyes from him.

"Man named Farraday says his son's gone missing."

"What's he think happened?"

Lasko shrugged. "Last time they saw him was at breakfast Monday. He said he was going over to Shakespeare's birthplace. In Henley Street."

"*Monday?* This is *Wednesday*. They don't seem in much of a hurry to find him."

Shaking his head, Lasko hitched himself up on the edge of his desk. "The reason they didn't report it was apparently this kid—he's nine—has a way of wandering off. That is, he's independent, I take it, and I also take it from some of the things the sister said—one of the sisters, that is—"

"Hold on, Sammy, you're losing me in the thicket of these relations."

"Okay. There's the father, James Farraday—" Lasko retrieved a small notebook from his rear pocket and leafed through it. "James, the father; there's a stepmother, Amelia-something, funny name; a sister, Penelope; another sister, no, stepsister with another funny name—I don't think I wrote it down right—Bunny Belle? Bunny Belle is the woman's daughter by another marriage and I wouldn't mind disappearing with *her* from Monday to Wednesday, let me tell you; or, to tell the truth, Amelia's not half bad—"

Given his own recent reflections, Jury's patience was not even dented. He was a patient man, in any event. He waited for Lasko to stop looking sourly at his own secretary for not having some of Bunny Belle's qualifications.

"They're an American family?"

"Who the hell else stays at the Stratford-bloody-Hilton except auto conventions? Inside, you'd think you were in New York. You ever been to New York, Jury?"

Lasko had been going on about the States ever since Jury had arrived that morning. It was a love-hate relationship. Lasko was dying to go to Miami and the Florida Keys. But he hated some of the brassy Americans he'd run into. Jury said no, he'd never been to the States, and Lasko stuck a toothpick in his mouth and went on. It danced as he talked.

"Like I said, this boy—name's James Carlton Farraday—likes to go off on his own. When they were in Amsterdam, he wandered off for hours—"

"Hours isn't two days. What were they doing in Amsterdam?"

"Tour. They're with one of these tour groups. In Paris he was gone for over twenty-four hours. Local police found him asleep in a church pew. Weird kid, right?" Lasko shrugged. "The girl, Penny, implied that he wasn't all that keen on his family."

"You mean she thinks maybe he's run away? That would be bloody silly in a foreign country."

"The kid's independent, like I said. Or they said."

"Well, what leads do you have?"

"None." Lasko looked gloomy, then looked hopefully at Jury. "I just thought maybe you—"

Jury shook his head, but smiled as he said, "Uh-uh, Sammy. I just came down here for a visit. This is your patch, not mine."

"But this guy Farraday is over at the Hilton raving away about Scotland Yard. I told him I could handle it, that it wasn't Scotland Yard's sort of thing, and that only made him madder. He's *American*, Richard. He's going to dance right into the bloody embassy and he's stinking rich and has a lot of influence, so he says." His tone growing steadily more wheedling, Lasko said, "Look, if it was a murder, I bet you'd do it."

And then he looked around the office, at the tables and chairs and secretary as if he might just scare up a dead body somewhere for Jury.

"It's not a murder, though, is it? And your Chief Constable's not asking for help from us—"

In a dramatic gesture, Lasko slapped his palms against his chest. "*I'm* asking—your old buddy, Sam Lasko. Look, all I want you to do is go along and have a talk with this Farraday. That's all. Just to shut him up."

Jury looked at Lasko speculatively and pocketed his cigarettes as he said, "Okay, but that's all, Sammy. I'm supposed to meet a friend for dinner tonight and I have—a few other things I want to do while I'm here, so don't expect me to do anything."

Lasko looked about as happy as Jury had ever seen him look, which wasn't very much. "That's great. These people think the only police in the whole bloody world are the FBI and Scotland Yard."

Jury picked up his notebook. "Not to worry. An hour with me and they'll change their minds."

5

The Farradays were sitting at a table in that part of the lobby of the plush Stratford Hilton sectioned off for the serving of drinks. Four pairs of eyes appraised Jury with varying degrees of interest.

Farraday himself, despite Lasko's report, seemed skeptical when Jury handed him his card. Lasko had probably made most of it up anyway, except for the initial report. Skeptical, but not unfriendly.

James Farraday rose and shook Jury's hand before immediately turning to collar a passing waitress. "What'll it be, Mr. Jury?"

Jury declined the drink. Farraday ordered it, anyway. Whiskey, no ice. "I know you fellas like your liquor warm, the Lord knows why."

"He said he didn't want any." The voice came from the shadows.

"Now, you just mind your business, Penny. He's just being polite." Farraday smiled at Jury with an assurance that Jury imagined informed everything he did.

The girl Penny he liked immediately, despite the way she sat there with her arms lapped over her thin body giving him a look hard as rocks. Penny was the green, not the ripe, daughter. Jury judged her to be around fourteen or fifteen, with a tawny, almost dusty look—as if she'd been walking down a dirt road barefoot. Freckles spattered like tiny drops of mud all over her face; long, straight hair the color of leaves underfoot; high cheekbones and light brown eyes flecked with gold, and tilted, giving her an intriguing, vaguely Oriental look. Her posture and her look told him she didn't know how pretty she was.

And no wonder. Sitting there between the stepsister and stepmother, both of them as ripe as peaches, with their highlighted blond hair and flushed cheeks—it would be hard for Penny Farraday to think she was anything but plain. The mother wore a white sundress with plenty of cleavage and a lot of strain across the breasts; the girl was dressed in a halter and shorts, hot-pink. They matched the lipstick she was running her small tongue over at the moment.

"This's my wife, Amelia Blue; that's Honey Belle, there, my stepdaughter."

The only person who seemed to be under a strain was Penny. And perhaps Farraday, himself, though he was the sort of man who'd probably rather die than show unmanly anxiety. But his voice did. "Look here, what're you fellas going to do about Jimmy?"

Jury took out his notebook. "Get some more information for one thing, Mr. Farraday. Sergeant Lasko says you last saw him on Monday morning."

"Correct. Said he was going to that birthplace."

"He often went off by himself?"

"Well, he *surely* did," said Mrs. Farraday— Amelia Blue—in an accent that ran like molasses. It went well with the rest of her. Jury bet the girl talked the same way. Both of them looked thick and ready to be poured. "You just got to keep a *leash* on James Cahlton." And here she shot her husband a hard glance.

"He likes to go off, see. We're always having trouble with him, the way he goes off, never says a word." Farraday took a deep drink from what looked like a triple whiskey. "It's hard to keep up with him." There was a hint of pride in his voice, and he looked around, almost as if he expected the boy to come walking in. And his face grew sad. Farraday tried to laugh, but it came out as more of a strangle. "We lost him for hours in Amsterdam—"

"You're with a tour group, Mr. Farraday?"

"Correct. Honeysuckle Tours."

What names they thought of. "And the rest of your group's here at the Hilton?"

Farraday shook his head. "No, no. That's not

the way Honeycutt—he's in charge of the whole thing—runs it. He fixes it so's different people stay wherever they've a mind. Listen, I wouldn't take one of them two-bit tours where thirty folks get herded on some piss-poor, broken-down bus and run all over creation. And let me tell you this ain't cheap. I'm paying—"

"The inspector ain't int'rested in all that, sweetie," said Amelia Blue, giving Farraday's arm a little shake, but smiling at Jury as if she knew what he might be interested in.

"How many others are with your group, then?"

Farraday counted on his fingers. "Besides us, there's six. Eleven altogether, including Honeycutt. He's over at the Hathaway or one of them other English hotels. Me, I like my conveniences. Can't imagine sharing a bath with someone else. We're Americans, you know—"

I'd never have guessed, thought Jury. "What part, Mr. Farraday?"

"Me and Penny and Jimmy—that's my boy— we're from Maryland." He pronounced it as two syllables. "Garrett County. Amelia Blue and Honey Belle—Amelia's my second wife and Honey Belle's her daughter—they're from Georgia. That's where Honeysuckle Tours has its offices, in Atlanta. Fella over there gets the tour together and this Honeycutt, he's a Brit, he runs things from this end."

"Are you sure your son mightn't be with one

of the others on the tour? Apparently, you've been together for some time—"

Amelia Blue got all girlish and giggly: "*Too* long, you ask me."

"Was your son especially friendly with someone?"

Honey Belle, who had done nothing all the while but fix Jury with her empty blue gaze and chew on a strand of yellow hair, finally decided to talk: "Jus' that crazy Harvey Schoenberg's all."

The voice utterly destroyed the illusion of wanton womanhood. The tone was flat, nasal.

"What was it about this Schoenberg he liked?"

"Harv's into computers," said Farraday. "And Jimmy's a right smart little fella, got a mind like a computer, I think."

"Stupid stuff." Honey Belle yawned, stretching her arms up elaborately and then clasping her hands behind her head, in case Jury'd missed anything.

"Anyway," Farraday went on, "he wasn't with Harvey. We've checked. We've gone and checked with everyone on the tour. No one's seen him."

Farraday coughed and got out his handkerchief. Jury realized, and with sympathy, that the cough merely disguised a threatening bout of unmanly tears. Farraday's eyes were glazed over as he stuffed his handkerchief back in his pocket, leaned across the table, and pointed his finger at Jury.

"Now look, here. I can get the American embassy, you know. So, what're you fellas going to do?" The man was used to doing business by means of hard-nosed threats, Jury imagined, but in this case, it was all facade: Farraday was really worried. Which was more than could be said for the others, except Penny. She hadn't said much, but she was very tense.

"Everything we can, Mr. Farraday. The Stratford police—Sergeant Lasko—are very capable—"

Farraday banged his fist on the table. "I don't want no piss-poor local *po*-lice on this job. I want the best, hear?"

Jury smiled. "I only wish I were. But we'll certainly do what we can. We'll need your cooperation, all of you."

A handwritten invitation couldn't have got a glossier smile out of Amelia Blue. "Well, now, you most certainly do have that, Inspector."

"He's a superintendent, didn't you hear him say?" said Penny, looking around the table as if they'd all got rocks in their heads.

That didn't put Amelia Blue off. "Well, whatever. I'm sure he's just *wonderful*."

There was a sort of gagging sound from Penny Farraday.

"Did your son have any money with him?"

"Yes." Farraday looked uncomfortable, as if he'd supplied the boy with the means of escape.

"Oh, not all *that* much; just in case he's out and needs a meal...," he ended, weakly. "He's nine. Boys are very spirited at nine."

"And at three," said Penny, counting her fingers, "and at four, five, six, sev—"

"Now that'll be enough from you, miss," said Amelia.

Penny melted back into silence and shadows.

"What does your son look like, Mrs. Farraday?"

"James Cahlton's my *step*son." She seemed to have to sort through some file of faces to bring James Carlton's to mind. "Well, he's so high"—her hand went out to measure off a few feet of air—"dark brown eyes and brown hair. He wears glasses. Like Penny, here. They both got 'stigmatism."

Jury turned back to the father. "Any distinguishing marks at all?"

Farraday shook his head.

"What was he wearing?"

"Blue shorts and his Pac-Man T-shirt and Adidas."

"Do you have a picture of him?"

"Well, there's one on the passport. Snapshots we took, we don't have developed yet." Farraday drew the dark blue passport out of his pocket.

Jury put it in his notebook and stood up. "Okay, Mr. Farraday. I don't have any more questions at the moment. I think I'll send someone along to have a look at his room. In the meantime, I wouldn't worry too much. Kids have a way of going off. And after all, this is Stratford-upon-Avon, not Detroit." Jury smiled. "Nothing ever happens in Stratford."

That, of course, was a lie.

6

Penny Farraday had, somehow, managed to cut through the lobby and make it to the front of the Hilton before Jury. She was waiting for him on the walk.

"I come out here because there's some stuff I want to tell you and I don't want them listening, especially that Amelia Blue. Come on," she was tugging at Jury's sleeve, "across to the park."

She made a death-defying sprint across Bridge Street, where the traffic shot over the bridge in an endless wave, before separating at the crosswalk.

"Let's set," she said, dragging Jury down on a bench positioned near the bronze figure of Shakespeare.

The river was choked with swans and ducks, streaming up to the banks for their lunch. A knot of children, probably on one of the last school outings of the year, was feeding them from bags of breadcrumbs hawked precisely for that purpose, like peanuts at the zoo. In the middle distance was the Memorial Theatre. Whoever had designed the Stratford Hilton, which was placed across the street and in view of the theatre, had cleverly designed it to match the theatre's modern lines, thereby binding them together in the tourist's mind. The day was golden, the sky an enameled blue. Jury didn't mind sitting here at all. He took out his packet of cigarettes.

"Gimme me one of those." Her words were a command, but her tone was uncertain. She expected to be refused. He gave her one.

She looked at the cylinder with such surprise he wondered if she'd ever in her life smoked before; he couldn't believe she hadn't. He held the match for her and it took her several puffs to get the cigarette going. She held it between thumb and forefinger, puffing it that hectic way of the amateur.

"He ain't our daddy, you know. Jimmy's and my, I mean. He kind of adopted us," she added, grudgingly.

Jury smiled at that "kind of." Still, he was surprised. Certainly the woman hadn't shown a mother's concern, but he thought Farraday had shown a father's. "No, I didn't know. Only that his wife wasn't your mother."

"*Her?* She sure ain't. Mama's dead, too." From a rear pocket of cutoff jeans she pulled a worn leather wallet from which she took a snapshot, black-and-white and creased, as if it had been handled a lot. She passed it to Jury. "This is

Mama." The sorrow in her voice was weighted like lead. "Her name was Nell."

The young woman—she seemed very young—stood in the shadow of a tall tree, but even in the bad light of the setting, he could see the straight hair and the bones of the face were Penny's. She stood there stiff and straight and not so much as the ghost of a smile on her face, a subject refusing to please the camera.

"I'm sorry, Penny." Jury handed the picture back. "What happened to her?"

Carefully returning the snap to its plastic sleeve, Penny said, "She died six years ago. I remember the day she packed her bag and left. She said to me and Jimmy, 'Honey, I got to go away for a while. Mr. Farraday, he'll look after you.' See, she worked for him; he liked her a lot and she him, I think. And she said, 'Now don't fret yourself; it may be a long while, but I'll be back.' Only that wasn't true. She never did come back." Penny lifted her head and looked out across the river, Jury thought past everything— the willows, the swans surfeited with crumbs and scudding against the bank, the brilliantly colored little pleasure boats moored at the edge. "She died of a wasting disease. That's what they told us. But Jimmy and me never did find out what that wasting disease was. I guess it don't make no difference. I guess you could say anything you die of's a wasting disease."

Jury said nothing, only waited for her to go

on. "Boy, was she pretty! You can't tell it from that picture—"

"Yes, you can. She looks exactly like you."

Astonishment was stamped on her face. Her light eyes seemed to refract some of the gold of the day. "Ah, *go* on. . . . No one ever looks at me with them two around."

"Some people have no taste, then. What about your real father?"

She dropped the butt of her cigarette on the ground. "I guess he died too. I don't think him and our mama was married, if the truth be known. Maybe I knew him. I don't remember. But Jimmy, he never . . ." This was brought out on a deep sigh, and in the words there was not a trace of reproach. People make mistakes, her tone seemed to imply.

"So He ups and marries this Amelia Blue, and sure as God made little green apples, her and Honey Belle think we're just bastards. Oh, they don't say it out loud; they wouldn't dare; their eyes say it. You just can see it in their eyes every time they look at us. That Honey Belle, there's words for what she is where I come from. I was born in West-by-God-Virginia—you can tell, I don't talk good—and what we call girls like that is just plain c-u-n-t—if you'll excuse my language—I trust I ain't shocking you. In West Virginia we got all kinds, so maybe we got c-u-n-t too, but I swear to almighty God with my hand on my heart"—and not to be thought a liar she placed it there—"that we ain't got it with a capital C. *That* had to come slithering up from Georgia. Now we live in Maryland," she added indifferently. "You can just see the boys around Honey Belle. They drop like flies every time she twitches that ass of hers down the street. I used to have me a boyfriend once." She sighed. It was not hard to imagine what happened to the boyfriend. "I know you think I'm jealous and I don't deny it. My God, you seen them shorts she wears? Practically up to her armpits. Well, you got to allow as how you know what I mean about Honey Belle."

Jury had to allow as how he did.

"And that Amelia Blue, she ain't no better. Two peas in a pod. It makes me sick the way she messes with men. There's this Englishman on our tour that I bet my life she's been fooling with—"

"Who's that, Penny?"

"Chum or Chomly. But it ain't spelt that way. First name's George. He's good-looking all right. Nearly has Amelia and Honey Belle wetting their pants. What I wanted to tell you was—you'll have to excuse me bending your ear this way—I think Jimmy might've run off."

"Run away, you mean? But surely not in a foreign country."

"You don't know Jimmy. 'James Cahlton,' she calls him. I swear, all those people down South have these stupid double names, so Amelia Blue

has to make them up for us too. She calls Him
James *Cecil* as if one name's not enough for any-
body. I ain't got a middle name, thank you,
Lord." She looked up at the sky. "We lived with
James Farraday for four years before he married
Amelia. He's okay, I guess. . . . He's in coal.
Owns most of West Virginia and western Mary-
land. And hotels. Got a big summer hotel in
Maryland. That's where our mama worked.
Waitressing and stuff. Jimmy was hardly a baby
when we came there."

"I think Mr. Farraday's really worried about
your brother."

"Yeah, well, maybe. If only He hadn't gone
and married *her*. Or I should say *them*. First time
we seen her bouncing up the drive we wondered Miss Dolly Parton wasn't honoring us
with a visit, all that blond sheep's hair and
boobs out to here. She tries to make me not cuss
and tries to make Him think she's all la-di-da
when you can just *tell* she's trash. She's always
got someone over—some *man*—sitting on the
front porch—*veranda,* she calls it—drinking beer
and fanning herself like she was born on a plan-
tation. You'd think she was Scarlett O'Hara. I
wouldn't be surprised to see her rip the curtains
off the windows and yell, '*Tomorrow* is another
day!' That woman's as phony as a three-dollar
bill." Here she looked at Jury from beneath the
smooth curtain of her long hair, obviously hoping he'd agree.

"Go on with what you think happened to Jimmy." He offered her another cigarette. That seemed to please her immensely.

As she puffed away again, she said. "You got to know Jimmy. He's different."

Jury could well believe it.

"Jimmy started working on this project of ways to get rid of Amelia Blue and Honey Belle. It wasn't nothing simple, like putting frogs in their beds and short-sheeting them. Jimmy, he's real smart. He talks good, too. He decided you don't get nowhere in this world if you don't talk good—you know—like politicals, that sort. What he did was, he got all of these books out of the public library on poltergeists—you know. Spirits that make noise and throw stuff around. Steven Spielberg made a movie of it. You seen it?"

Jury shook his head.

"Then he told Honey Belle the house was haunted. She's the biggest coward God ever made. *Then*—I don't know how he did it—he made chairs move and glasses walk all over the cupboards. He made drawers open and all sorts of stuff. Scared them both shitless but didn't get rid of them." She smoked her cigarette, looking hard at the riverscape. "Jimmy's got you might say an elaborate mind—like him."

Incredibly, she seemed to be studying the bronze statue. "Shakespeare, you mean?"

"Yeah. You ever read him? I just *love* that

Shakespeare. I must of been to see *As You Like It* three times already. We had to read that in school and I learnt all the speeches." She ground out her cigarette. "Listen, you just got to find Jimmy."

He doubted she was used to pleading. . . . Hell, another hour or two on this case wouldn't kill him. The bell of Holy Trinity Church drenched the air with its tolling of noon. "Come on, Penny. Let's go over to Shakespeare's birthplace and ask a few questions."

"Me?" That she would be helping out in a police investigation changed the sad look utterly. Light seemed to gleam through the dust of the freckles as she walked beside him, across the brilliant green of the grass toward Henley Street. Still, she continued her odyssey of life with her stepmother and -sister. "It's like a steambath around that house. Jimmy's the only thing brightened my life. Well, I've decided in the last two days I ain't going back there. I'm going to stay right here and try and marry up with a duke or earl or someone. I like Him okay, but I just can't stand those two no longer. Not being around that house with all them tits and asses. You wouldn't happen to know any, would you?"

Jury was not sure whether she was referring to tits and asses or dukes and earls. "As a matter of fact I do know an earl." He smiled.

"No shit!" She stopped and looked up at him, her face all wonder.

"No shit," said Jury.

The birthplace was a pleasant, homey, half-timbered building of Warwickshire stone whose door was nearly flush with Henley Street. Outside that nearly sacred door, a double line of pilgrims waited, impatient parents and quarrelsome children licking iced lollies. Jury wondered how many of the people there actually read Shakespeare, but he had to admire them and their willingness to take genius on faith.

"It looks like the lines to *E.T.*," said Penny, morosely. "It must be a hundred people ahead of us."

"I think maybe we can navigate round the crowd. Come on."

The woman at the door, wearing the emblem of the Shakespeare Trust, observed Jury's warrant card with a kind of horror, even after he had assured her that nothing was wrong. She still looked up at him uncertainly, as if afraid he might drag into the birthplace, not only the girl at his side, but also the effluvia of Criminal London, which would be left behind to cling like a patina of dust to the precious collection within.

There was as much of a crowd inside as out. Jury showed the picture of James Carlton Farraday to the guardian of the rooms downstairs, but met with no response. They made their way upstairs, to other small and cheerful rooms—white-plastered and solid-timbered. The furnishings were Elizabethan and Jacobean, but none of them, unfortunately, Shakespeare's (so a guide upstairs was informing the pilgrims), except for the old desk from the Stratford Grammar School, where young Will had had to endure no end of terrors. The desk was marked and pitted.

Jury approached an elderly gentleman, another guardian, who was dispensing information to a disheveled young woman in shorts and sandals, regarding the leaded glass window, where the names of the famous of other centuries had been cut with diamond rings. The woman in sandals slapped away.

Jury produced his identification. "I wonder if you might have seen this boy in here on Monday morning."

The gentleman seemed astonished that someone would be inquiring into the whereabouts of anything except furniture and windowpanes. Especially that Scotland Yard would be the inquirer. When Jury showed him the picture in the passport, he shook his head.

"We get so many schoolchildren on holiday and, especially now, with term nearly over. Well, you know, one schoolboy begins to look like another. There are so many of them and they ask so many questions . . ." He went on in this vein, prompted to overexplain out of some conviction that Scotland Yard might think he had this particular schoolboy locked up in the oak trunk beside him.

Jury handed him a card, entering the number of the Stratford police station above the Scotland Yard number. "If you should remember anything, anything at all, give me a call."

The guide nodded.

The result was the same in the souvenir shop on the other side of the gardens, where the pilgrims were buying up all sorts of Elizabethan memorabilia: place mats, cut-outs of the Globe Theatre, postcards and pictures and pendants. None of the harassed salespeople recognized the picture of James Carlton Farraday.

Jury and an unhappy Penny were now standing looking down the central walk, bordered by flowers. There were quince and medlar trees and the summer air was pungent with the fragrance of flowers and herbs.

"I read in this little book they got all the flowers here that Shakespeare talks about in his plays. I wonder if they got rosemary." She pushed her long hair behind her ear. "That ain't a flower, is it?" Her look at Jury was very nearly inconsolable. "That's for remembrance."

7

James Carlton Farraday was tired of being kidnapped.

He did not know who he had been kidnapped *by*, or where he had been kidnapped *to*, or what he had been kidnapped *for*.

At first, he had not minded, but now he was bored. He was tired of the same room—a little one way up high like a garret. His food was delivered on a tray slipped through an oblong that had been cut into the door. Probably he was in a tower, although there were no rats. There was a cat, though. It had determinedly squeezed through the opening in the door. It probably wanted to see what it was like, being kidnapped. The cat, a gray one with white paws, had curled up on the foot of the iron cot and gone to sleep. James Carlton shared his food with it.

The food was all right, but he would have preferred bread and water, at least for a couple of days. He didn't think it quite fitting that he be served Jell-O (or whatever they called it in England) out of a little tin mold with a rose design on top. He himself hated Jell-O, but the gray cat loved it and licked it all up. The rest of the food was not bad, even if its method of delivery was a little unconventional. Not at all like his old nurse bringing a tray to his room back home, bringing things like runny boiled eggs and dry toast. Boy, was he glad to be rid of *her*.

James Carlton had read every book ever written (he supposed) on kidnappings of one sort or another. People stuck up in towers, or carted away to Devil's Island, or thrown in dungeons, or captured by Zulu tribes, or lowered into viper pits, or stuffed into trunks of cars. He was obsessed with kidnapping because he was pretty sure that was what had happened to him and Penny years ago. And he wasn't even sure that it was J. C. Farraday who had done it. Actually, he thought not. J. C. did not seem to be the sort. Amelia Blue, now, she'd take anything not nailed down, and that included babies, only Amelia Blue wasn't around then. Probably he had looked so cute lying in his carriage outside the Sav-Mor, someone had just snatched him up and run off. He thought it pretty stupid of Penny—who was usually very smart—to believe that story about their mom having died of that strange disease. She hadn't, of course.

The police were still looking for him (and Penny too, he supposed) after all these years, though they had certainly kept it quiet. His real mother and father would never give up looking for him, he knew. One thing that had made it so hard for him to be found was because Amelia Blue and J.C. made him wear these big eyeglasses. When he was a baby the kidnappers must have dyed his hair. For he had seen the picture of his mother, and she had light brown hair like Penny.

James Carlton had been going along with all this in a good-humored way for years. He had never said a word about being kidnapped, or asked why they didn't let him go home. But now he was getting mad. To be kidnapped once was bad enough. Twice, and somebody better have a pretty good reason.

The gray cat was napping on his chest and he exhaled deeply. Inhaling and exhaling could make it go up and down. Finally, the cat got disgusted and jumped down.

Beyond thinking of ways to escape, there was nothing to do. Naturally, there were no pencils or pens in the room because of the danger of his writing notes and sending them out of the window for passersby to find and report to the police that there was a boy in the tower.

But James Carlton always carried the stub of a pencil in his sock, because he knew how important it was to have a writing implement. More important than a weapon, really. It was necessary for sending out SOS's to the police, or for leaving messages behind when people moved their captives from place to place.

He had often toyed with the idea that if he did not decide to become a baseball player when he got older (his father, he was sure, was a baseball player), he would probably become a writer. A foreign correspondent. And writing was also something to do to keep your mind busy when you were bored.

Around the walls a number of pictures had been hung, all of them quite stupid, of Irish setters or cows in meadows. He took down one of the pictures of cows and a shepherd and lay on the bed with the picture overturned, resting on his knees. From his sock he took his pencil and continued his diary. It wasn't very interesting writing this, but it had to be done in case his kidnappers moved him and the police came looking for him. With painstaking care he had already managed to work a clue into the picture itself by carefully removing the backing paper and the picture and tearing out the heads of the shepherd and the cow and exchanging them. It had been very difficult and meticulous work and had taken him upwards of two hours, as he had no glue and had to position the heads carefully. They kept sliding around beneath the glass. Finally, he had used spit for glue and was pleased with the result. No one who lived here would notice because no one ever looked at their own pictures. But Scotland Yard would see it and know that it was some sort of clue and look at the back of the picture.

At the top of the backing paper, which he had restuck round the frame, he had written *James Carlton Farraday* in as fancy a script as he could. He went on now with his diary:

7:13 Brekfs't Egg, bacon, cereal

He printed this in small neat letters, under last night's dinner, which had been served him at 6:22 exactly. They had not taken away his watch.

Now he went on to his escape plans, listed in the order in which he would probably try them:

1. Pretend sick—when food comes, moan and groan
2. Grab his/her wrist through door slot when tray sits down
3. Figure out way to get out of window. Lower cat?????????

James Carlton replaced the picture on the wall and did some deep knee bends. It was important to try and keep fit. After that, he shadow-boxed around the room and over to the bed. He threw a few punches at the cat, all the while doing his fancy footwork. The gray cat rolled over on its back, made a few desultory swipes at his fist, got bored and rolled over on its side. James Carlton shadow-boxed off.

He stopped when he heard the footsteps. At the sound of the tray clattering down on the floor, James Carlton put plan number one into action. He lay down on the floor and began to moan and groan horribly.

8

The Dirty Duck's dining room—that somewhat more luxurious part of the pub called the Black Swan—was crowded with diners who were getting in drinks and dinner before the seven-thirty curtain. The terrace spilled customers onto its steps; in the saloon bar of the Duck there was barely room to lift a glass.

Melrose interrupted his discourse on the Schoenberg theory to taste the wine their dark-haired waitress had just poured. When he nodded, she filled their glasses and whisked off.

"That's the stupidest theory I've ever heard. Pass the mustard," said Jury.

"I haven't finished. *Then* he says that maybe Shakespeare had to kill Marlowe, because if he didn't, *Marlowe* would kill *Shakespeare*." Melrose shoved the mustard pot toward Jury, who dotted his steak-and-kidney pie all over with it. "And then he keeps bringing up Shakespeare's sonnets on this Ishi—"

"What the hell's that?"

"His computer."

"You mean he's carrying a *computer* around Stratford?"

Melrose cut into his roast beef. "Of course. He couldn't have a conversation without it. He says there are already computers that you can talk to. Just talk to. Maybe I could get one for Agatha. It could sit with her when she comes over to Ardry End for tea."

Jury smiled. "We haven't met in three years."

"You'll keep it that way if you're smart. She'll track you down, never fear. When she can spare time from the Randolph Biggets."

"Who're they?" Jury held out his glass for a refill.

"*Our* American cousins. Hordes of them. Fortunately, I've managed to avoid them. I've taken rooms at the Falstaff and left dear Agatha and the Biggets to the Hathaway. Americans go for it; mock-Tudor and mud-and-wattle."

Jury smiled. "Not quite. Very expensive place. 'Rooms at the Falstaff'? How many did you take?"

"All of them." At Jury's raised eyebrow, he added, "Well, I had to, didn't I? Otherwise, there'd be Biggets spilling out of all the windows. I simply told Agatha I'd got the last room. Which I had, in a manner of speaking. There're only eight or nine, anyway. Are you going to do anything else about this boy who's gone missing?"

"There's not much else I can do at the moment. I went with his sister, Penny, to Shake-speare's birthplace. He was supposedly on his way there when he disappeared—but no one remembered seeing him. Anyway, it's Lasko's case."

They ate in silence for a while. Jury's mind turned from missing boys to other matters. "You never met Lady Kennington, did you?" He doubted his overly casual tone would fool Melrose Plant.

"No. I only saw her that one time, you remember. Attractive woman."

"I suppose so. She's living in Stratford."

"Oh? You know, she reminded me of Vivian Rivington."

It hadn't occurred to Jury, but Plant was right. There was a resemblance between the two women. Plant was looking at him rather too closely; Jury looked away. The thought of Vivian Rivington still nettled. "Have you heard from her? Is she still in Italy?"

"I get some sort of postcard of a gondola now and again. She said something about returning to England."

There was a short silence. "Pass the bread," said Jury.

"How romantic. I mention Vivian and you say, 'Pass the bread.'" Melrose shoved the basket across to him.

"Oh, God," said Jury, looking toward the door.

Melrose followed the direction of Jury's gaze. The dining room was thinning out, as one table after another left for the theatre. Standing in the doorway was a rather corpulent, sad man who was looking their way. He said something to the hostess and threaded his way through the departing diners.

"Speak of the devil—" Jury tossed down his napkin.

Detective Sergeant Sammy Lasko stood there looking, Jury thought, insincerely apologetic. "Trouble, Richard."

"Sit down and have some wine or coffee. You look beat."

Lasko shook his head. "No time. Looks good though," he added, peering longingly at their plates.

"It was until you walked in. Something else about the Farraday kid?"

Sad shake of the head as Lasko turned his bowler hat in his hands. "'Fraid not. It's a little worse."

Plant and Jury exchanged looks. "I daresay I'll be attending the theatre by myself this evening," said Melrose, glumly.

"Look, Sammy . . ." Jury sighed, giving in. "What is it this time?"

"Murder," said Lasko, still eyeing the cut of beef.

They both stared at Lasko, and then at one another. Finally, Jury said, as he got up, "Give me my ticket and meet me in the bar during intermission."

Sam Lasko looked at Jury reproachfully. "I don't think we'll have the answers by the middle of *Hamlet*."

"Neither did Hamlet. Come on, let's go."

"Gwendolyn Bracegirdle," said Lasko, looking down at the spot in the ladies' toilet where the body had recently lain. He handed the pictures taken by the police photographer to Jury, together with Gwendolyn Bracegirdle's billfold. "It was a mess."

In the bulb's white glow, the face of Gwendolyn Bracegirdle wore an expression of clownish surprise. When Jury opened the billfold, a little waterfall of credit cards spilled down in a long plastic sleeve: Diner's Club, Visa, American Express, one for petrol. And there was quite a bit of money, at least two hundred pounds.

"Not robbery," said Lasko, eyes in the back of his head. He was scrubbing at the dirt in the walk with the toe of his boot. "Why would she have been walking out here by the public toilets at night?"

"When did you find her?" asked Jury, looking down at one of the photos, at that awful expression on the murdered woman's face—as if she had been almost laughing when the first cut came. Awful, given that the head was nearly severed from the body. As if slicing her from ear to ear wouldn't have done the trick, there was another deep cut beginning below the breast and running in a vertical line to the pubic bone. The blood must have gushed; in the photos, it looked as if it had dried, as on an artist's canvas, so thickly it might have been put on with a palette knife.

"A couple of hours ago. Been dead, according to the doctor, since late last night. All this"— Lasko gestured with his outstretched arm at the blood-painted world—"happened around midnight, or close to."

"And someone *just* found her? The church is overrun with tourists in July."

"Not using the toilets. There was an Out of Order sign outside." At Jury's look, he shrugged. "They really *were* out of order, apparently."

"All that blood. The killer must have been covered in it—"

"Sure was. We found an old raincoat tossed in a dustbin. We're checking it for prints, but it's one of those slick ones. Also, cheap. Kind you could get anywhere. Hell to trace." Lasko stuck a toothpick in his mouth, and held up a small, white card, illuminated by his torch. "How about going along with me to the Diamond Hill Guest House? Have a word with the landlady?"

"I told you before, Sam, this isn't my—"

Lasko cut Jury off by asking, "What do you think of this?"

It was a copy of a theatre program for *As You Like It*. Across the bottom, two lines of poetry were carefully printed:

> *Beauty is but a flower*
> *That wrinkles will devour.*

"So what do you think, Richard? We're checking the original for prints. But for openers: think she wrote that?"

"No."

"Me either. Looks more like a message to us."

Resolutely, Jury handed back the copy. "You, Sammy. To you. I've got to go back to London, remember?"

But Sam Lasko still had his pièce de résistance to offer. "I think you'd better come along."

"Sammy, no one's asked for our help."

"Not yet. But I'm sure Honeysuckle Tours maybe could use it." Lasko rolled the toothpick around in his mouth. "You know, the tour the Farraday kid was on." Lasko put the theatre program back in its envelope. "So was Gwendolyn Bracegirdle."

Sam Lasko let Jury stand there for a while and digest this information before the sergeant took out his notebook and flipped through the pages: "It's a terrific name, isn't it? Just makes you think of the Old South and Tara and all that stuff. You been to America, Jury?" The question was rhetorical; Lasko didn't wait for an answer before going on with his list.

"This guy runs it, Honeycutt—probably that's where they got the name—we've been looking for him ever since we found her. He's been bouncing around all over Stratford. Anyway, we got the Farradays on this tour and, according to J.C., who's only just barely speaking, there were four others, leave out them and Honeycutt: a Lady Dew and her niece, Cyclamen—talk about names!—George Cholmondeley, he deals in precious stones; and Harvey L. Schoenberg—"

"Schoenberg?"

"You know him?"

"No. But the chap I was having dinner with does."

"That so?" Lasko put his notebook away, and attempted to steer Jury down the path and—presumably—toward the Diamond Hill Guest House. "What I was thinking was, maybe after we get finished with this Diamond Hill—"

"We?" But Jury knew he'd go along.

So did Sam Lasko. He didn't even bother answering. "—I thought maybe you could go along and have a look into the Arden—that's Honeycutt's hotel—and have a word with him or find out where the hell he is—"

Jury turned in the dark walk. "Sammy, I told you before—"

Sam Lasko shook and shook his head, holding out his arms almost heavenward. "Richard. Look at that mess back there. You think I don't have enough to do—?"

"No, I don't."

They were walking up the alley that made a shortcut from the theatre through old Stratford to the streets skirting the town, lined with B-and-B's like avenues of beeches.

"*Casablanca.* Now there was a film. You've seen it, haven't you?"

Jury stopped, lit a cigarette, and said, "Don't get the idea this is the beginning of a beautiful relationship, Louie."

9

Mrs. Mayberry, who ran the Diamond Hill Guest House, did nothing to correct Jury's impression of women who ran Bed-and-Breakfast establishments.

"I don't know, do I? She was on one of those tours. Had the room right at the top—small, but cozy. Hot-and-cold and bath down the hall. Seven pound a night it cost her, and full English breakfast, VAT inclusive." The police might have been there for no other purpose than to rent Mrs. Mayberry's rooms.

Jury knew what the full English breakfast would be: tinned orange juice, cornflakes, one egg, bit of bacon if you were lucky, watery "grilled" tomato. Only Oliver Twist would have the nerve to ask for seconds.

"The last time you saw her, Mrs. Mayberry?" asked Lasko in his sleepy voice.

"Six-ish, I guess it was. Come back to the house for a wash before dinner. They usually do." They were climbing the stairs now, preceded by the landlady with her ring of keys. The

police photographer and fingerprint man
brought up the rear. "Here we are, then." Mrs.
Mayberry stood aside and pushed open the
door. "Shocking, it is." Jury assumed she was
commenting on the murder and not the state of
the room, which was small and rather barren.
"Terrible thing to happen." But the comment
seemed to be aimed less at Gwendolyn Bracegirdle's death than it was at the nerve of a Diamond Hill Guest House lodger giving the place
a bad name.

The room was on the top floor and the tiny
dormer window seemed designed to keep out
the summer breezes rather than to let them in. A
bed—really more of a cot—with a chenille
spread flanked one wall. A washbasin sprouted
from the other. Besides this there were only a
chintz-covered slipper chair and an old oak bureau. On the top of the bureau, Miss Bracegirdle's things were neatly arranged: a couple of
jars of cream, a comb and brush, a small picture
in a silver frame. Jury was standing in the doorway so as to keep out of the way of Lasko's
team, and thus couldn't see the face in the picture. But it struck him as sad, this attempt to
carry some small part of home around with her.
The rooms of a murder victim always struck
Jury in this way: perhaps because he had been
trained to observe objects so closely, they became sentient to him: the bed ready to receive
the weight of a body, the looking glass to see the

face, the comb to touch the hair. The presence of Gwendolyn Bracegirdle clung to these things like scent, even though she'd been in this room for only a few days.

Before Lasko started going through the drawers, he said to Jury. "Why don't you have a little talk with the landlady?" His eyes were imploring.

"Sure," said Jury. As long as he was here . . .

Mrs. Mayberry was fortifying herself with a cup of tea in the breakfast room-cum-parlor. One weak bulb glowed thriftily in the rose-shaded lamp on the sideboard. The sideboard told him he'd been right about breakfast: cereal boxes sat in a row beside a brace of tiny juice glasses that would provide one large swallow apiece. There were three round tables, each with its complement of mismatched chairs, and each with its centerpiece of mismatched condiments. Mustard for breakfast?

"On the Saturday she came," said Mrs. Mayberry. "Came at the same time as the man and wife in Number Ten. I don't mean together; she didn't know them."

"Did she get friendly with any of the others while she was here?"

"Well, now, I don't know, do I? I don't mix with my guests. In the morning I'm in the kitchen. One's got to look sharp these days to see breakfast's done proper and the rooms cleaned and so forth. We've got to do the cooked breakfasts up in advance, the eggs and such, as they *will* all come in at the same time, won't they? Even though we serve from seven-thirty. Spot on nine they all troop in—" She pushed her frizzy hair off her forehead and shook and shook her head. "My checkout time's eleven and the linen's got to be changed—"

Feeling as if he were being interviewed for a job, Jury cut in on her: "I'm sure it's very difficult. But there must have been someone here who passed the time of day with Miss Bracegirdle."

"Maybe she talked with my Patsy who waits at table and does some of the upstairs work. Called in sick today, she did, and I felt like sacking her."

Jury interrupted this recounting of domestic problems: "Did she take any phone calls while she was here?"

"No, none I know of. You might ask Patsy that. She answers a lot of the time."

The guest register, which Mrs. Mayberry had been rather proud to bring in from the little hall table, was open in front of Jury. Looking down at the small but florid signature of Gwendolyn Bracegirdle, he said, "Sarasota, Florida."

"That's right, Florida." She fingered the bottle of catsup. "I get lots of them from Florida. Of course, lately there've been a lot of British *going* to Florida. It's ever so cheap, they tell me. I wouldn't mind a bit of a holiday myself, but as you can see, there's so much business here that I never do get away—"

"We'll have to talk with the other guests here, Mrs. Mayberry. There's evidence that Miss Bracegirdle was with someone when she met with her, ah, accident."

Her face was a sheet of horror. "Here? You're not saying—"

"Not saying anything. We're just gathering information."

But the thought that she might be giving bed and breakfast to a murderer was, to her, not the issue: "The Diamond Hill Guest House isn't going to be in the papers, now is it? Nothing's ever happened here . . ."

It brought back to Jury his own consoling words to Farraday that nothing ever happened in Stratford.

"We try to keep things out of the papers."

"Well, I should certainly think the Diamond Hill Guest House shouldn't have to have its good name besmirched . . . It certainly wouldn't do my business any good. Even with travel so expensive these days, the Americans still come. Stratford's just as popular, *more* popular, than ever. In tourist season, it's—excuse my language, it's hell."

Jury gave her a level look. "It certainly was for Miss Bracegirdle."

*   *   *

"We'd like you to sign this, please, madam," said Lasko, who came down a few minutes later. The Scene of Crimes man had left with a suitcase full, presumably, of the effects of Gwendolyn Bracegirdle. "We've sealed off her room, of course."

"Sealed!" Mrs. Mayberry was indignant. "But I've got people booked into that room."

Blood running in the streets of Stratford should not interfere with custom.

"Not until we've had time to give that room a much more thorough going-over." Lasko pocketed the pen with which she'd signed the release form.

"Isn't that a fine thing, then! What am I supposed to tell them, I'd like to know?"

Mildly, Lasko said, "Why not tell them the last roomer got herself sliced up with a razor?"

The broad steps and the lobby of the Royal Shakespeare Theatre were packed so tightly with playgoers, Jury bet there wasn't an empty seat in the house and that some of the Standing-Room-Onlys had already ferreted out his empty seat and were making for it right now.

Melrose Plant was squashed into a corner of the bar that catered to the Dress Circle crowd.

He handed Jury a cognac and said, "I had the foresight to order the drinks before the curtain went up."

Jury drank the small portion in one or two swallows. "Curtain's going down. Come on."

Despite Plant's mumbled complaints about missing the second half of a very good *Hamlet*, it was clear he was only too happy to thread his way through the crowd after Jury, even though he didn't know where they were going, or to whom.

The *Where*, he discovered, was straight Stratford-upon-Avon stuff: the Arden Hotel.

The *Whom* was something else again.

10

"My friends," said Valentine Honeycutt, his intense look suggesting he would love to number Jury and Plant among them, "call me Val."

"Mine," said Melrose, call me Plant."

"*Oh!*" exclaimed Honeycutt, with a small shiver of excitement. "You go by just a *last* name? You must be hideously important!"

"Hideously," said Melrose, as he put his silver-knobbed stick across the table by his chair.

Valentine Honeycutt redistributed the folds of the daffodil ascot that bloomed in the V of his candy-striped shirt done in pencil-thin lines of green and yellow. His blue linen jacket must have been chosen to complement his sky-blue eyes. All in all, looking at him was like taking a stroll through an Elizabethan knott garden. He crossed one perfectly creased trouser leg over the other in the way of one given to conversing largely through body language. "What can I do for you gentlemen? Care for a smoke?" His hand made an arc with his silver case.

"Mr. Honeycutt," said Jury, "we've come to inquire about this tour you manage—"

"Honeysuckle Tours, that's right. Sort of a play on my own name and also because our office is in Atlanta, Georgia. Honeysuckle vines and all that. Every June for six weeks it's London, Amsterdam, the English countryside and London again. Stratford's always on the agenda. Americans dote on it. The theatre and all."

"Six weeks. Sounds expensive."

"It is."

"I'm afraid I've some rather bad news for you."

Honeycutt's whitish-blond eyebrows arched over his innocent blue eyes as he reared back slightly. He looked a little like an angel who'd stumbled on a hole in his cloud. "Has something happened?"

"Afraid so. To one of your group. A Miss Bracegirdle—"

"Gwendolyn?"

"Yes. A rather serious accident. Miss Bracegirdle's dead."

"*Dead!* Dear God! I know she was complaining about pains in—but you said 'accident.'"

"She was murdered."

Honeycutt seemed pulled by invisible hands from the chintzy chair in which he had arranged himself like a bouquet. "*What?* I don't understand—"

It seemed easy enough to understand to Jury.

"What were you doing last night, Mr. Honeycutt?"

Honeycutt was looking from one of them to
the other with such seeming lack of comprehension that Jury wondered how the man ever managed a railway guide. "Me? Well, I was at the
theatre. Like everyone else, I imagine."

"With anyone?"

"No. No, I went by myself. *As You Like It*. It
was . . ." The voice trailed off.

Jury was afraid for a moment he was going to
tell them the story by way of establishing an
alibi. "We thought perhaps you might be able to
throw some light on Miss Bracegirdle's
friends—anyone in Stratford she knew, that sort
of thing."

He found his voice long enough to say, "No.
No."

"How about on the tour itself?"

Honeycutt was smoking with quick little jabs.
"Oh, God, this is going to be hell for the tour.
Wait until Donnie finds out—that's my partner.
In Atlanta."

Jury wished people would leave off thinking
about business. "Whom was she especially
friendly with on your tour? Did you know her
well yourself?"

That brought a very quick response. "No! I
mean, no better than the others."

"When did you last see her?"

Regaining a bit of his composure, he said, "Well . . . yesterday, I think."

"You don't keep close tabs on your clientele."

"Lord, no! Sometimes I don't see them for *days* at a time. Honeysuckle is not at *all* the usual sort of tour. For one thing, a person must, quite honestly, be just this side of filthy rich to take it—"

Jury interrupted. "Including Miss Bracegirdle?"

Honeycutt had revived enough to give a little snort of laughter. "*Of course* Miss Bracegirdle."

"But she was staying at a B-and-B. The Diamond Hill Guest House."

"Oh, that makes no odds. She chose to. That, you see, is another unusual thing about our tour. One thing we do *not* do is book the whole lot into some perfectly dreadful hotel months and months in advance. *Our* clientele choose their own place, with guidance from us. And we, of course, do the scullery-girl drudge-work" (he began to twinkle again) "and arrange the bookings. Old Gwen wanted to get down to the rough-and-tumble, wanted to think she was staying with the plain folks . . . well, you know what I mean. In other words, she didn't want the Hilton—much too American, she said. So we fixed her up at that rather seedy little Bed-and-Breakfast." He shrugged. "Yet she was quite rich. Millionairess, unless I miss my guess. Oh.

Is that too hideously sexist?" He turned the twinkle on Melrose Plant.

"Hideously."

"Well, all I can say is Gwen had lolly up to her earlobes. One must, as I said. Honeysuckle's nearly as expensive as the QE-Two, believe it or not. We advertise only in *quality* magazines. *Country Life* over here. In the States, *The New Yorker.* Believe me, we're not one of those tarted-up tours where they shove twenty or thirty on a broken-down bus. We have a coach, of course, but a very new one, wide seats and a bar for food and drinks. We offer all sorts of options if one gets tired of being bused about. For example, if one wants to motor from London (or anywhere else) I see to a car rental and make sure the little dear is properly stuffed behind the wheel and point him in the right direction. We have a very *personal* approach, and I think more of my fellowman than to pretend an hotel that has tinned tomato soup for starters is serving *haute cuisine*. We're strictly five-star Michelin when it comes to food."

Jury smiled. "Because you think more of your fellowman, Mr. Honeycutt?"

"More of four thousand quid, then," said Honeycutt, returning Jury's smile with a glowing one of his own. "And more of myself than to be always herding this lot on and off old bangers of buses and leading them in and out of museums and galleries, installing them—and me—in

roach-ridden hotels where fish and chips consti-
tute the comestibles, or one of those absolutely
ghastly islands in the Caribbean where the flies
revolve but the fans don't and the only palms
are the ones stuck out for tips—no, no, my dear,
no thank you. We strive for some balance between dependence and independence for our
customers. They are free to spend their time as
they like, buying out the shops or spending ten
hours over dinner or whatever. The Farradays,
for instance—the lovely man is loaded—
wouldn't be caught dead without their mod
cons and pools and bars—"

"That's another thing. When did you last see
the Farraday boy?"

"James Carlton? Umm." Honeycutt studied
Melrose Plant as he set his mind to this problem.
"I believe it must have been Sunday or Monday.
Monday, yes. Why? Little beggar scarper,
again?"

"You're not surprised?"

He hooted. "He's *always* wandering off and
coming back with his clothes torn as if he'd been
doing battle with a school of sharks. He'd win
hands down. The daughter, Honey, she's rather
a deluxe little piece . . . Farraday hasn't got the
police looking for James Carlton?"

Jury nodded. "Last time they saw him was at
breakfast on Monday morning."

"It *was* Monday morning, I think. Early on
Sheep Street. Well, I didn't take any special note

of him; he's always round and about. Ask his sister, Penny. She's the only one he really talks to. In some language of their own," he added without much interest.

"Had you seen Miss Bracegirdle with anyone, then? What about this George Cholmondeley? As he was unattached—"

"Well, he certainly wasn't attached to Old Gwen, my dears." He bridled at the suggestion. And then added with a bit of a pout, "Amelia Farraday might have been a bit more his type."

"Harvey Schoenberg?"

"My, you *have* got us all dead to rights, haven't you?"

Jury smiled. "Just asking. How about Schoenberg? He's also got money, I take it?"

"Has his own computer business. Have you any *idea* how much money there is in computers? Of course, Gwen knew him, but I can't tell you if she was *with*—" Suddenly he seemed to have twigged it: "Look here, Superintendent. You're not suggesting Gwen was done in by one of *our*—?" Immediately he dismissed the notion. "Preposterous."

"No, I wasn't suggesting anything. Just casting about." Jury stood, and Melrose Plant gathered up his stick. "But Honeysuckle Tours has some stiff competition."

With that comment, Honeycutt pretty much wilted on the vine. The yellow ascot withered, the linen jacket drooped. "Oh, dear."

* * *

"Hideous," said Melrose Plant, when they were on the sidewalk again.

"I agree," said Jury. "How would you like to go along tomorrow and see the Dews? They're staying at the Hathaway. I want to talk to this George Cholmondeley."

"Lady Dew," said Melrose Plant. "Why is it I get stuck with the titled ones?"

Jury smiled. "No less than you deserve. That Honeycutt. Wonder what his partner in Atlanta is like?"

Melrose stopped in the dark street where the little sign of the Falstaff was just visible. "Don't know. But I imagine you could lay them end to end."

11

Chief Superintendent Sir George Flanders, one of Warwickshire's Division Commanders, was a tall man who towered over Lasko, but not over Jury, although he tried. Sir George refused to sit down, refused even to remove his raincoat, as if these indications of impatience might stir his police forces to taking stronger action, might hurry them along toward a solution, even a spurious one. At least that's the impression he gave, standing there glaring at the huge map of Stratford in the incidents room and talking about the American Embassy. He had made it quite clear that nearly twenty-four hours had passed without Lasko's coming up with a solution. It was not a matter he wanted to have to report back to the American consul.

Two matters. "A murder and a missing child," said the Chief Superintendent for the umpteenth time, as if he might, like Macbeth's witches, exorcise these dreadful occurrences through constant repetition. "A murder and a—"

"There's no reason to think the boy won't turn

up. He's run off before. I shouldn't be a bit surprised if he didn't walk into the Hilton in the next few hours." Lasko checked his digital watch as if to make them all stop here until his prediction proved true. "No reason to connect up the two—"

"Of course not," said Sir George, with a rather dreadful smile at his detective sergeant: "What it might be is *two murders*." His look was lethal.

Lasko, perhaps in some attempt to match Sir George's own disinclination to undress, was still wearing his bowler hat. It was pushed down over his forehead. "Now it's certainly early days to be—"

"Early days? Tell *that* to the American Embassy. These are *Americans*, man," he repeated, as if Lasko hadn't got nationalities sorted out. "It is only by the grace of God and the British press that we've kept the damned thing quiet this long. I shudder to think how the *American* tourists in this town would react—" And he shuddered, as if a demonstration might spur everyone on.

Jury refrained from suggesting that English blood ran just as red and that Americans were no strangers to rape, assault, murder, and kidnapping, although he had to agree that the American press was spot on and fulsomely reporting these events almost before they happened.

As if reading Jury's mind, Sir George

swiveled his head—a very handsome gray-
haired and -moustached one—around to Jury.
"And after I finished with the consul, I was on
the phone a goodish time talking to your
chief . . . what's his name?"

"Racer."

"Yes, Racer. You know, we didn't call on your
CID for assistance, Mr. Jury."

"I know," said Jury, smiling. Lasko would
have to explain his recent attachment to the
Stratford CID.

From under his hat, Lasko said, "I asked Superintendent Jury to go talk to the Farradays because Farraday was raising such hell about
country cops and where in the bloody hell was
Scotland Yard? They think the only police force
in the world outside the FBI is Scotland Yard.
They never heard of the French Sûreté, or the—"

"Yes, yes, yes, yes," said Sir George, his palms
raised to ward off a journey round the world's
police forces. "Mr. Jury's kindly lending a hand.
However—" Again he turned to Jury. "—your
chief's a bit upset you're involving yourself un-
officially—"

As Sir George went on to report Racer's comments, Jury simply tuned him out, having heard
Racer's comments so many times before.

Sir George seemed satisfied with having
made it crystal clear that the Warwickshire constabulary could still take care of its own manor.

Only then did he give Jury a reluctant nod. "He says you're to make sure you ring him."

"Very well." Jury was not to move an inch without instructions from Chief Superintendent Racer. He would certainly make it a point to call him one of these days.

Glumly, Sir George said, "Of *course*, there's a connection between this woman's being murdered and this boy. Got to be."

Jury silently agreed.

"Who else was on this bloody tour? And who runs it?"

Lasko leafed through the notebook lying on his desk. "Man named Valentine Honeycutt is the director—"

"Good God, these Americans do trick themselves out with florid names."

"He's not American," said Lasko. "He's British."

Sir George grunted. "Anyway. You talk to him?"

Without even exchanging a glance with Jury, Lasko nodded, and explained the operation of Honeysuckle Tours to his chief superintendent.

"What about the others?"

"Besides the Farraday family—there're five of them—a Lady Dew and her niece, and a George Cholmondeley—"

"Don't tell me *they're* Americans."

"No. Lady Dew and her niece have been living in Florida—"

"That's where the Bracegirdle person was from."

"Sarasota's not Tampa."

Again, Sir George grunted. "That the lot?"

"Then there's a Harvey L. Schoenberg." Lasko closed his notebook. "He was the one who seemed most friendly with the Farraday boy, but says he hasn't seen him for days. And none of them were particularly friendly with Bracegirdle, that I can tell."

"No evidence turned up so far," Sir George's heavy sigh made it sound as if the body of Gwendolyn Bracegirdle had been found two weeks ago, rather than twenty-four hours. "Except this." He picked up the theatre program. "What on earth could the murderer have meant by this?"

> *Beauty is but a flower*
> *That wrinkles will devour.*

Sir George shook his head. "What is it?"

"A poem," said Lasko, wiping his nose with a large handkerchief.

Sir George turned a cold, cut-glass blue gaze on Detective Sergeant Lasko. "I *know* it's a poem, damnit. My question is, *what* poem and *why?*"

Lasko shrugged. "Sorry."

"I don't like it. It looks like a message. I don't like messages to the police."

Neither did Jury. That piece of paper made his

blood run cold, because it was a signature—just the sort of little love letter psychopaths like Jack the Ripper enjoyed writing to police.

The trouble was, such murderers seldom stopped with signing their names only once.

12

Cyclamen Dew had about her that sham-supernal, self-deprecating air of one who, not born to sainthood, had gone out to get it.

Seated next to her aunt, the Dowager Lady Violet Dew, in the bar of the Hathaway Hotel, Cyclamen Dew (an unappealing, angular woman) had been putting Melrose in the picture—a large tableau filled with separate scenes of anguish, disaster, missed opportunities, and dreams turned to dust, as the result of having been in constant attendance to Aunt.

Lady Violet was a silent, glaring old lady who sat hunched in her chair during this lengthy recital, wheezing in her lace and locket and black lawn dress.

"So as you see," said the niece Cyclamen, with her hundredth sad little shrug, "you take us as you find us."

Melrose knew no other way to take anybody, and hoped her statement was a wind-up so he could introduce his own topic. But apparently not. Cyclamen was merely changing gears.

Another huge intake of breath and she continued: "One small dream of mine was always to have gone into service—"

"You wished to be a waiting-maid . . . ?" asked Melrose innocently.

She fairly tinkled with laughter. "Oh, my dear man, *no! I mean*, of course, the Holy Sisterhood. But as you see . . ." A small wave toward the Dowager Lady Dew, who kept her own black button eyes riveted on Melrose. And then Cyclamen perhaps bethought herself, or perhaps thought of her aunt's rather considerable fortune, and changed her tune. "But, then, of course, could there be a Higher Calling than what I am doing for Aunt?"

Aunt made the only sensible reply, Melrose thought, that a person could: "Get me a gin."

"Now, Auntie Violet, you *know* what Dr. Sackville says about that! You are *not* to touch spirits. A nice cup of tea, now—"

The ebony stick banged smartly against the table leg. "I don't give a good goddamn what that lecherous old fart says—" Here she turned to Melrose. "—he's laid every woman in Tampa—" And to Cyclamen: "I said a gin. Make it a double."

Melrose started to rise with the intention of getting the drink, but Lady Dew fanned him back to his seat. "Never mind; she'll get it. What's your business here, young man?"

Cyclamen knew when she was licked and,

blushing, headed to the bar. Melrose was a bit
surprised that she didn't make the journey on
her hands and knees.

"I'm making a few inquiries for the police.
No, I'm *not* police, but Superintendent Jury of
Scotland Yard asked me to come here."

Her heavy black brow, beneath tendrils of
gray hair, furrowed. Her dentureless gums receded like a dent between the hooked nose and
protruding chin. Lady Dew seemed in an immi-
nent state of collapse, physically. Mentally was
another story. "If somebody's gone and killed
that tart Amelia Farraday, I wouldn't be a bit
surprised."

Melrose was. "You mean you've some reason
to suspect that somebody on your tour is in danger?"

"You just said police, didn't you?"

"Ah . . . yes. But, actually, it's to do with a
Gwendolyn Bracegirdle—"

"That dope. What's she been up to? Can't
imagine she's been in on the old slap-and-tickle,
not with *her* shape. That Amelia, now—"

Cyclamen was back, glass in hand. "Really,
Aunt, you mustn't go saying things about—"

"Oh, put a sock in it. Say what I like. I buried
three husbands; lost and made two fortunes; got
arrested five times; tried to climb Nelson's pillar
and danced stark on the grass outside the Crystal Palace; fornicated with most of the princes of
Europe—"

Cyclamen shut her eyes. "Don't excite yourself, Aunt."

"I only wish I could. So what's all this about the Bracegirdle person?" she asked, drinking off half of her gin neat.

"Gwendolyn?" asked Cyclamen, eyebrows shooting up. "What about her?"

"I was just telling Lady Dew. Miss Bracegirdle has met with an . . . accident. Rather serious. She's dead."

Although Lady Dew did not seem too perturbed, Cyclamen was irritatingly aflutter, asking all sorts of broken questions which Melrose finally had to cut across. "No. It was murder."

That rather delighted the old woman who seemed to take her excitement like her gin, neat; but the younger one did a fair imitation of a Camille-like swoon.

"Oh, stop it, Cyclamen. If the woman's dead, she's dead." Then she turned to Melrose with a fresh interest. "Sex crime, was it?"

"The police are not sure."

"Well, I could tell them. Wasn't any of that with old Gwendolyn. She wouldn't know it if it walked straight up to her and barked. Believe me, I can tell."

When she leaned closer and dropped her arthritic and beringed little hand on Melrose's knee, he got it off by offering her a cigarette. While Cyclamen reminded her of Dr. Sackville's instructions regarding smoking, Lady Dew lit up.

"What can you tell me about the rest of the people on this tour?" asked Melrose, sliding his chair out of reach.

"Nothing."

"Plenty."

"*Really*, Auntie—"

"Shut up."

"But common gossip!"

"So what?" Had the bullet-spray of these responses been actual ammunition, Melrose would have died where he sat.

Smoking and wheezing, the old lady inched her chair toward Melrose. "You've seen that Farraday crowd. That Amelia's twenty years younger than him if she's a day. Obvious why he married her." Lady Dew drew a shape in air. "Daughter's just as tarty as the mother. It was quite a scene in Amsterdam, both of them rubbing up against that Cholmondeley person— you met him?"

Cyclamen wore her Patience-on-a-monument expression as she dropped her hand over her aunt's clawlike fingers. It was quickly shaken off.

"Don't look so innocent, Cyclamen, with what you were getting up to—"

"*That's a lie!*" the niece fairly bellowed, reacting appropriately for the first time. Her raised voice had caused the few other customers in the dark bar to turn. She then rose from her chair, announced that she had a dreadful headache, and marched off, presumably to her room.

"Hell it is," said Lady Dew, fanning herself briskly as she watched the niece go. Melrose wondered if the old lady's goading wasn't in direct proportion to the young one's martyred acceptance of it. "Buy me another gin and I'll tell you the works," she said happily.

"With pleasure," said Melrose.

"Cholmondeley and the Farraday woman were absolutely *glued* together. Saw them with my own eyes out on the terrace of that hotel in Amsterdam some of us were staying in." Lady Dew was clearly enjoying the story as much as the gin, which Melrose had set before her. "Amelia Farraday went on and on about how she'd been an *actress* when she met him. Let me tell you, *that* one never saw the inside of a theatre dressed in anything but feathers and fans." Her own black fan went faster and faster as the gossip got hotter.

"Vertically or horizontally?"

The fan stopped. "What?"

Melrose smiled. "You said you saw them 'glued together.' I was only wondering—"

Lady Dew snickered, snapped her fan shut, and hit him on the knee. "You're my kind of person. Ever cheat on your wife?" she asked, lowering her voice.

"I can't do. I'm not married." As her beady eyes sparkled, he reverted to the other topic: "Were you implying that your niece was interested in Mr. Cholmondeley? She seems much too—spiritual."

She flashed him a dark and bladelike smile. "Don't be a damned fool. *Her?* She's—" She changed the subject. "But that Farraday's no fool," she said, continuing with her story. "Made a fortune in coal. Strip mining. He knows some racy stories, I'll give him that. Limericks especially. I collect them. Know any?"

Melrose wondered if it were possible to keep the woman's mind on murder. "A few. But much too mild for you, I'd wager."

"Try me." The cavernous mouth collapsed and recollapsed in her version of a salacious sort of smile. "You know, you ought to come to Florida, young man. Get a bit of tan in those rosy English cheeks of yours."

"Unfortunately, I burn. Lady Dew—"

"Not to worry. We could go round the tracks. I could teach you my betting system. We could dump old Cyclamen, have a crackerjack time." She slapped his knee. "Don't think I can't move it. I can get to the windows before those bookies can—"

Melrose interrupted. "There's nothing I'd like better. But tell me—what about Gwendolyn Bracegirdle?"

"Colorless wench. All that talk about 'Mama

this' and 'Mama that.' Bracegirdle *really* had problems."

"She must have been especially friendly with some of the others."

" 'Friendly' is the word. AC/DC if you ask me." When Melrose only looked puzzled, she slapped his thigh and said, "You know. Men, women, and maybe the odd animal. She liked that Schoenberg chap with his crazy machine, but he didn't seem interested. Of course, he's so busy with his computing he hasn't time for fooling around. Not a bad egg, just silly. Wears shirts with those little alligators and awful bow ties. Talked a lot to the Farraday boy, James-whatever. The boy's the only one who can understand him. Me, I couldn't understand a word of it. Better things to do than fool around with that, 'ey?" She winked.

"Actually, the Farraday boy's missing."

She shrugged. "Makes no odds. He's always wandering off. Frankly, I think it's because he can't stand the family. Who could blame him? Neither can his sister, that Penny. Oh, he'll turn up, never fear."

"And you can't think of anyone on the tour, or in Stratford, for that matter, who would wish Miss Bracegirdle dead?"

"Heavens, no. She was harmless enough, I suppose. Of course, I don't know what she's been getting up to in Stratford. Haven't seen the woman for two or three days. That's one thing I like about this tour. We can pretty much go our own way, no one the wiser." Here she winked at Melrose.

. . . Who hastily rose, collecting his cigarette case and stick. Lady Dew and murder did not seem at all convivial. He felt the need of a little talk with Jack the Ripper. "Thank you for your time, Lady Dew."

"Call me Vi—oh, hell's bells, here she comes, the Lady with the Lamp."

Cyclamen, headache better, was crossing the room, looking horribly determined. "Din-dins, Aunt Violet," she fluted.

"Get me a gin."

With a gracious farewell, Melrose left where he'd come in.

13

Jury found George Cholmondeley in the Welcombe Hotel's dining room, his corner table bathed in a gauze of light streaming through the high window behind him.

"Mr. Cholmondeley?"

The handsome man looked up at Jury.

"Superintendent Jury, Scotland Yard CID. Could I have a word with you?"

Cholmondeley smiled a little coldly and indicated the chair across from him. "I expect if I said no, you'd turn right around and go away."

Jury returned the smile with a genuine one of his own. "But you're not going to say no, are you? Sergeant Lasko has already talked to you."

Cholmondeley nodded. "Care for something? Coffee? Tea?" he asked quite civilly. Dressed in an Italian silk suit, a watery taupe shade that matched his eyes. Cholmondeley was a very handsome man. The fair coloring, the artistically thin fingers now engaged in boning a trout, the languid air which was vaguely decadent—all of this would appeal to women. Iced in a bucket beside him was a Château Haut-Brion.

The man was clearly not a middle-class clerk who had to save up for a year for a two-week holiday in the summer.

Jury said no to the coffee and tea, and to the wine, when Cholmondeley raised the bottle to replenish his own glass. "How well did you know Gwendolyn Bracegirdle, Mr. Cholmondeley?"

"Hardly at all. Certainly I was distressed to hear what had happened to her, though." The distress did not seem to affect his appetite. He ate the fish with considerable relish.

"What were her relations with the other members of your group?"

Cholmondeley looked up, vaguely puzzled. "Well, I couldn't say. She spent quite a lot of time with the Dew woman. The younger one, that is." He broke off a bit of roll, dabbed it with butter. "Why do you want to know *that?*"

Jury shrugged. He did not want to put Cholmondeley on his guard any more than he might already be. "Well, we've got to start somewhere."

Cholmondeley frowned. "Then why not start with the seamier side of Stratford underlife? The Most Wanted list? Why start with Honeysuckle Tours? And, incidentally, why Scotland Yard? I should think Warwickshire has an adequate constabulary."

"It's got a very good one. But to answer your questions. Stratford hasn't much of a seamy side. Of course, we're checking all possible sources—but one is inclined to believe that murderers are usually close to home."

"Perhaps, but we're none of us home, are we?" Cholmondeley polished off his fish, took out a cigarette case. "What I mean is, I'm surprised you would think—as you apparently do—one of us had something to do with it."

Lasko must have made more of an impression than, perhaps, was good. "It's early days for us to be thinking much of anything, Mr. Cholmondeley—"

Cholmondeley gave him a sharp glance that said he didn't believe a word of this as he lit his cigarette and then leaned back, apparently all at ease.

"—but surely the members of a group with whom Miss Bracegirdle had been at pretty close quarters for a month could throw some light on her character, personality, habits, friends . . . ?" said Jury.

"Not I. I barely passed the time of day with the woman." And he gazed off through the light-saturated window as if the only thing either of them had on their minds was a stroll through the hotel's gardens.

"Who did you pass the time with, then?" asked Jury pleasantly. "Mrs. Farraday, maybe?"

That got just the reaction Jury wanted: massive annoyance. The man had been too glib, too unconcerned up to now, and consequently, too confident. "I beg your pardon? And who's been saying that?"

The arrow must have struck home. Otherwise, Cholmondeley wouldn't have assumed that *anyone* had been saying "that." Having seen Amelia Farraday, it would be hard to believe Cholmondeley wouldn't have had some attraction for her and she for him. A little tour romance, when Farraday was looking the other way. Jury smiled. "No one, really. It's just that Mrs. Farraday is a very attractive woman."

"Also a very married one."

"Does that mean anything these days?"

Cholmondeley did not answer, just kept looking, turned to one side, out the window.

Jury dropped the subject of that possible liaison. "Did anyone on the tour appear to dislike Miss Bracegirdle?"

"Not to my knowledge. To me she wasn't the sort one likes or dislikes, really. I found her a bit too . . . effervescent. You know. Too much talk, too many bubbles."

"So you *did* talk to her?"

"Well, of course. Chatter about the weather, that sort of thing." Impatiently, he flicked cigarette ash toward the glass tray.

"Were there any bad feelings among certain members of the group?"

"Only the usual spats and minor jealousies. What one might expect."

"I've never taken a tour. I don't know what one might expect."

"You're being awfully literal, Superintendent."

"I never saw a murder solved through metaphor."

Cholmondeley sighed heavily. "Oh, very well. Naturally, there was trouble with the boy—there always is with children. The Farraday boy—James Carlton, I think his name is—liked to wander off."

"Um. He seems to have wandered off again."

Cholmondeley did not seem especially surprised. "They're used to it, the parents. Had a hard time rounding him up once or twice. Funny boy." Cholmondeley shrugged the problem off; it was none of his. "And then of course there is the generally quite hideous Lady Dew. Lady Violet Dew."

"I haven't had the pleasure."

"No pleasure, I assure you. She lives in Florida and comes back once a year to whip her relatives into shape. They must love her having control of the pursestrings."

"She confided in you?"

"She confided in *everybody*."

"What about Schoenberg?"

Cholmondeley poured himself another tot of wine. "Queer duck. Really, it's rather hard talking to him, since he talks mostly in computerese. RAMS and ROMS and so forth. But he gets on like a house-afire with the Farraday boy. A very intelligent lad, actually; I'm not surprised he outsmarted his parents so often."

"Farraday?"

"What about him? Pleasant, I suppose. Too loud for my tastes. A lot of money which he probably made too quickly and doesn't know how to spend fast enough. The two daughters loathe one another, of course. I feel rather sorry for the ugly duckling."

"Do you mean Penny?"

He raised an eyebrow. "Well, obviously not Miss Peaches-and-Cream." And he looked at Jury as if his taste in women probably matched his taste in ties: dull.

"Have a bit of trouble with Honey Belle?" Jury smiled.

"Now you think I'm a child molester?"

"I was thinking of the molesting coming from the other side."

At least Cholmondeley offered a more genuine smile than before. "A little, yes."

"But not Miss Bracegirdle? She didn't give you any trouble?"

Cholmondeley gave him a look of absolute astonishment. "Well, good lord, no. You mean no one's twigged that but me?"

"Meaning what?"

"Gwendolyn is—I mean was—as they say in

America, queer as a three-dollar bill. So's Cyclamen Dew."

It took Jury a moment to digest this information. "Is that why, do you think, they went off together at times?"

Cholmondeley obviously enjoyed having just thrown a spanner into the works. "If Miss Bracegirdle had a heavy date, it wasn't necessarily with a man. That's all I'm suggesting." He looked out of the window again, unconcern written all over his face. "Certainly, I'm not trying to implicate anyone."

The hell you're not. "How are you so sure of all this, Mr. Cholmondeley? I mean, that both are—were—lesbians."

"My dear fellow," said Cholmondeley, in that has-your-naiveté-no-bounds tone, "you'd only got to *look* at them—"

"My first sight of Gwendolyn Bracegirdle wouldn't have told me that," said Jury coldly.

Cholmondeley had the grace to redden slightly. "No, I realize that. Well, besides . . ."

"Yes? Besides what?"

"It sounds terribly vain, I realize, but . . ."

His voice seemed to drift away on the tendril of smoke from the cigarette he stabbed into the ashtray. And he had the grace to blush again.

"Neither of them was interested in you, you mean?"

Cholmondeley nodded. "Look, I don't mean

to suggest I've got the charisma of Mick Jagger—"

Jury smiled. "A bit long in the tooth now, isn't he? Mick Jagger?" He couldn't decide whether he liked Cholmondeley or not. The man kept slipping through his fingers, like the fine Italian silk suit Cholmondeley was wearing.

"True. I wasn't trying to charm anyone. Women like me, that's all. But those two didn't even know I was alive."

It seemed a simple statement of fact: women liked him. Jury wasn't surprised. He only wondered how much advantage Cholmondeley took of that fact. "That doesn't extend to Amelia Farraday, though? Or even her daughter?"

He snorted. "For God's sakes, I don't need to rob cradles. And as for Mrs. Farraday, I really don't see as how it makes any odds—"

"It might. I appreciate your sense of delicacy; however, it could be important—your relationship with Mrs. Farraday."

"Why? What's that got to do with anything?"

Jury shrugged. "I guess that's for us to decide."

"I wish I knew what the hell you're getting at. Should I have my solicitor present?"

Jury bestowed upon Cholmondeley a perfectly innocent smile. "Beats me. Should you?"

"You know, Superintendent, you're an unnerving man. You don't *seem* to want to intimidate me. And yet—"

"I'll bet your nerves can hold up under pretty strenuous questioning. Look, Mr. Cholmondeley,"—Jury leaned forward, shoving aside the napkin-covered basket of rolls—"I'm simply asking for your help. I don't give a damn what was going on between you and Mrs. Farraday" (if Cholmondeley believed that, he was a fool) "but I think it's important we understand the relationships between the people on Honeysuckle Tours—"

"Terrible name, isn't it? And have you met Mr. Honeycutt, our guide? Our amanuensis?" His look at Jury was somewhat apprehensive, although he tried to hide it beneath this overlay of superciliousness.

"Yes. He didn't say anything about you."

Nor could Cholmondeley hide his relief beneath his offhand comment: "Guess I'm just not Honeycutt's cup of tea."

"Maybe. But why were you on the tour in the first place?"

That caught him off guard, as Jury meant it to. "I beg your pardon? Because I wanted a bit of a holiday."

Jury took from his pocket what appeared to be scrolls of paper, managing to give the impression that each had Cholmondeley's name at the top. "You're a dealer in precious stones?"

"Yes. It looks like you've a good deal of information there about me."

"This tour went to Amsterdam."

Cholmondeley frowned. "Many tours go to Amsterdam. *Most* tours that do this sort of London-Paris circuit. It's one of the easiest and nearest places on the Continent to get to. Directly across to the Hook of Holland—"

"Do you happen to have your passport handy, Mr. Cholmondeley?"

Now Cholmondeley looked utterly confused. Apparently ready to refute or refuse confidences about his new lady-love, this new line of questioning had taken him aback. He drew out his passport, tossed it on the table.

Jury looked at the visa stamps. The pages were full. Passing it back to Cholmondeley, all he said was, "Thanks." He returned the passport.

Cholmondeley sat there turning a silver knife over and over, looking at Jury. "I don't know what you're getting at. As far as this tour's concerned, all I can say is, we come from different parts of the world, have never met before, know nothing about one another—and you're making it appear that one of *us* is lurking about, waiting to get at the others." He tried to smile, but his smile seemed to break in two. Apparently it was a novel and most unwelcome notion: "One of *us?*"

14

Melrose Plant sat morosely in his seat in the Dress Circle wishing he were out there looking at a real bloody corpse rather than waiting for Hamlet to litter the stage with fake ones.

The theatre was as full as it had been last night. He was fortunate to have got a seat in the first row; he was damned if he was going to miss the second half again—

Was that his name being called? As he peered over the brass railing at the stalls, he also thought he heard the name echo from behind. The Memorial Theatre was supposed to be an acoustical marvel: his name seemed to be coming from all directions.

"Hey, Mel!"

Ah, yes. About a dozen rows up sat Harvey Schoenberg, waving frantically. Melrose returned the wave with a vague gesture.

"Melrose!"

Good God, there was Agatha down there, standing in front of her seat also waving, but with both arms, as if she were directing the lift-off of a 747.

Had he known she was coming to this evening's performance, he would have torn up his ticket. His attempt to ignore her only resulted in her trying harder to get his attention, and now the people around him were giving him chilly looks. Would his performance be competing with Hamlet's?

He looked again over the rail, and raised his hand in a sort of salute and wondered if those rather plump-looking people sitting either side of her, craning their necks upward, were a few of the Randolph Biggets. When he saw her cup her hands round her mouth, prepared to shout over the surge and sweep of heaven knew how many hundreds of voices, Melrose slid down in his seat. He blessed the houselights, which had just dimmed.

It was good, but then was the Royal Shakespeare Company ever anything else? Hamlet was not overly melancholic after the opening scene, Gertrude was wonderfully lascivious, old Claudius was a bit more sympathetic than usual. A little hard to have sympathy for Claudius. By the time the intermission arrived, everyone's nerves were on edge, on stage and off. Melrose was not looking forward to the ambush in the bar.

*   *   *

Since he had had the foresight to order his brandy before the play began, he didn't have to join the general crush, but managed to retreat back into a corner. There was a bow-tie bobbing out there somewhere; he got occasional flashes of Harvey, who was finally upon him.

"Can you feature it? All the time we were in that church—there she was lying out back." Harvey slashed his finger along his neck.

Rather tastelessly, thought Melrose, who inquired, "Did you know the lady well?"

"Hell, no. Just we were on this tour together." He shook his head sadly. "Poor Gwennie. Man, you could've knocked me over with a feather." Harvey polished off his beer as the lights blinked. "See you. I'm in the middle and I hate crawling over people."

Melrose thought he was safe for two minutes, but one was never safe from Agatha, who was bulldozing her way toward him. She could sniff him out as a terrier could smell a fox gone to earth. "Melrose!"

"Hullo, Agatha. Fancy meeting you here. How did you ever find the place?" She just stood there, looking horribly pleased with herself, and clearly waiting for him to ask her why. "Have you worked through the reasons for Hamlet's delay, or what?"

"You will never *guess* who's here!"

"You're dead right. Would you like a brandy? Or must you get back to the Biggets? *They*, I take it, are here." His lack of enthusiasm, he hoped, was noticeable.

"Close your eyes!"

"Close—? For heaven's sakes. No."

The pout started at her mouth and seemed to spread all over her face.

"Really, Agatha—" Whatever warning he meant to level at her was immediately stopped as he stared over her shoulder.

There was Vivian Rivington.

The only one of the three not perturbed by this meeting was Agatha, who stood there looking pleased as punch and taking full credit for Vivian Rivington's magical appearance as if she'd just pulled a rabbit out of a hat.

Vivian herself seemed both pleased and disconcerted, seeming not to know what to do with her hands.

Melrose solved her problem by embracing her. "My dear Vivian. What in the *hell* are you doing in Stratford? How did you get here? Why aren't you in Italy?"

Agatha answered for Vivian as she did for everyone. "She motored here from Long Pidd. Said when Ruthven told her where we were, she just decided to come along. She said—"

"—and she only speaks Italian now, and she's hired you as interpreter. I would appreciate it, Agatha, if—"

"The lights!" said Agatha, as they dimmed to announce the beginning of the next act. Afraid she might miss a minute of something she'd paid to see, Agatha had already started plowing her way back through the crowd.

"Let's get out of here, Vivian. Let's go over to the Dirty Duck and have a drink and a talk."

"But the play—" Vivian started to say.

"I'll tell you how it comes out."

Since nearly everyone in town was watching the second part of *Hamlet*, the Dirty Duck was not as crowded as usual.

He set their drinks on the table. "It's been three years."

Three years, and this wasn't the Vivian he had grown so used to. That one hadn't looked like this one. Where were the subdued twin-sets and skirts, the unrouged lips? The hair was the same autumnal brown with reddish highlights, but she had never worn it messed about on the top of her head that way, curls hanging down. He supposed it was devilishly fashionable. And she had never worn such a blinding shade of green before. Her dress was low-cut and clingy.

"Three years, yes." She took a packet of cigarettes from a purse of silver scales. "I came back to see about selling the cottage in Long Piddleton."

"Sell? Why?"

"I'm getting married."

The match burnt his fingers as he stared at her. "No."

"Yes."

"Well, where is he, then?"

"In Italy."

"What the hell's he doing there?"

"He's Italian." Short pause. "Oh, don't look like that. He's not a gigolo. He's not after my money."

Vivian had rather a lot of it.

"So you met him in Naples. How disgustingly romantic."

She shook her head. "Venice. And it *was* romantic. *Is*, I mean."

"Aha! Indecision."

She laughed. "No, not really. But why are you disturbed? After all, *you* never wanted to marry me."

Vivian's directness caught him off-guard. Was it something she'd picked up in Italy? The thing that got him about her was that she was a genuinely modest woman who could be, at the same time, straightforward. There was hardly any room to move in with Vivian. Nothing to stumble over, searching one another out in the dark. No play of sun and shadow. Vivian stood in the bright light of day.

"What are you smiling about?"

He quickly changed his expression.

"And what on earth are you doing in Stratford in July? You never went anywhere in summer, much less somewhere in summer, much less somewhere touristy."

"I still don't. But don't you remember—" He

stopped suddenly. Of course Vivian would remember Richard Jury. More to the point, Jury
would certainly remember *her*. Melrose was certain Jury's interest had been more than professional. And now there seemed to be this
Kennington woman lurking somewhere off-
stage . . .

"Remember what?"

"Nothing, nothing. I came because had I not
Agatha would have had her American cousins
trooping through Ardry End."

Vivian laughed. "You've always been too nice
to her, Melrose. And she's always been perfectly
dreadful in return."

"I'm *not* nice to her, and it's interesting having
someone perfectly dreadful about. You can prac-
tice reactions on them. It's sort of like being
goalie in a soccer game. Anyway, it's wonderful
to see you."

"Are you sure?"

Her eyes actually seemed to be twinkling at
him over the rim of her glass. What was she
drinking? Naturally, Campari and lime. Didn't
they all, over there? He knew he was irrationally
irritated with Vivian. Why had she come back
now, all Gucci'd up in that glittery green dress,
silky hair dripping down the sides of her face
like an Italian ice, and probably saying awful
things like *Ciao?* . . ."

"When are you leaving," he asked.

"Well, *thanks*. Might I just finish my drink

first?" She looked at him again with cool amusement. "I'm picking up Franco at Heathrow tomorrow. He's coming in from Rome."

Franco. Heathrow. Rome. It all sounded so terribly international.

"And then . . . well, if you're going to be here, I'd like you to meet him—"

"Do you want the wedding at Ardry End? It's probably big enough to hold his entire family."

"That's nice of you, Melrose." She still smiled. "Agatha will like him. He's a count."

"A *count?*" Really, this was too much.

"They have titles over there too; you're not the only one."

"I am not titled. I dropped all of that nonsense years ago. Had I known *that* was what you were after, maybe I'd have hung on to the earl and viscount and the rest of it longer."

She looked away. "Don't be absurd. I'm not 'after' anything, and you know it. He just happens to be a count, that's all."

"No one just *happens* to be a count." All Melrose could visualize was this black-caped stranger. "Can he see his reflection in a mirror?"

Now Vivian was angry, and rightly so, he thought. "Oh, for God's sake . . ."

Melrose slid down in his seat, grabbing at his neck, just to annoy her more.

Then he thought of the look on Sergeant Lasko's face. That's all Stratford needed at the moment. More bloodletting.

15

For a seventeen-year-old, Stratford-upon-Avon was not exactly Arcadia. No card clubs, no discos, no movies, not even any streetcorner activity. But Honey Belle Farraday could find the action if you put her down in a field of cows.

Tonight she was swinging down Wood Street as if it were the Vegas strip. And when Honey Belle swung, she swung—hips packed into Sassoon jeans; breasts, not exactly hidden beneath a white Indian cotton top about as opaque as a fogged-over pane; bangle bracelets, loop earrings, and gold chains. Underneath it all she was stark. Honey Belle went in only for necessities.

Stratford. What a one-horse town. Nothing to do but boring plays and boring sightseeing. You couldn't even get a decent tan lying around the Hilton pool. But she still lay around it, because it gave her a chance to show off the white swimsuit she'd bought in Paris—nothing more than a few sateen patches held together by string—that old James thought was scandalous. Who did he think *he* was kidding? It gave Honey Belle a real

kick to think her own mother was jealous of her.
Nearly killed her after she found her and old
James in the big bedroom at home, and Honey
Belle only wearing those flimsy babydolls—
well, they hadn't *done* anything, really. But
you'd never convince Amelia Blue of that.

She crossed over the roundabout and passed
the Golden Egg and looked in the window at
people stuffing themselves with eggs and pan-
cakes. Of course, she didn't *eat.* You couldn't eat
and have the kind of body she had, she thought,
passing fingers with plum-painted nails over
her washboard tummy. Flat. The television commercial for some Chinese food jingled in her
mind: *"Take care of your beautiful bod-y; take care of
your beautiful bod!"* Boy, and didn't she ever take
care of her bod. She sighed with pleasure at the
mental picture of herself, as two women with
shopping bags passed her. They must have been
forty-five, fifty, she thought, looking after them.
She wondered how anyone could live that long
and not kill themselves.

Honey Belle was scared of only one thing: losing her looks, getting old and wrinkled. She
could see her own mother's looks beginning to
erode, though she had to admit Amelia Blue did
a pretty good job of taking care of herself. Thank
God Amelia Blue at least once had been a real
looker; and thank God, too, her own daddy had
been tall and blond, a real lady-killer. She
guessed Amelia couldn't stand it anymore,

being second-best to his latest tart, and had finally had to dump him. Honey Belle giggled as
she wondered if her mother knew just how
much of a daddy's girl Honey Belle had been.

She passed the alleylike opening of a small
street crowded with little shops, thinking how
they'd kill her—Poppa James and Amelia
Blue—if they really *knew* about her, and what
she was doing for the money to buy stuff like
gold chains and Sassoon jeans. Dancing in a top-
less bar. Posing for a photographer friend who'd
tried a hell of a lot more with her than just taking pictures. It wasn't the sex Honey Belle liked;
it was the power. My God, the power it gave her
over men. Being up there on a platform with
those blue and pinky lights splashing over her;
or posing on couches and cushions in those *posi-
tions*. It wasn't the sex, no, it wasn't that. She
hated actually *doing* it. It was the making-men-
think-about-it. Think about doing it with *her*.
What made her own body tingle was watching
them watching her, was thinking about the men
who bought those pictures raking her with their
eyes. Her career was pretty well set. When
James talked about school, about her grades, she
nearly laughed in his face. She was either going
to be a model or it was going to be movies. . . .
Almost as if the thought of all those movie pro-
ducers after her had taken some concrete shape,
she heard feet behind her.

Honey Belle stopped in a dull pool of light

outside a small bookstore and lit a cigarette. The thin stream of smoke rose upward, evaporating into the blue phosphorescence of the streetlamp. She smiled. What she was actually doing was stopping the sound of her own clogs to see if the feet behind her stopped too. Because Honey Belle could tell when *she* was being followed even if you dropped her into the middle of a regiment of marching feet. And she was right. She had not seen, she had sensed, back there in the narrow alley of shops, a shadowy form, just standing, looking in a window. Until whoever it was saw her. And that was enough. Still smoking her cigarette she walked on. There was this underground place near the train station where she'd heard there was dancing, drinks, pot, and maybe even a couple of snorts of coke. Honey Belle could sniff out the action—she giggled at her own little joke, swinging along the walk.

But the giggle caught in her throat as the hand clamped down on her mouth and she felt the breath on her neck.

Oh, shit! was her last thought: *Come all the way to England just to get raped! And who'd'a thought it in this shitty little place*—but in those few seconds while her little brain was still connecting with the world beyond her body, she also thought, Why not? It was the kind of sex where you didn't have to do anything—and then there was that cold thing on her skin, her India shirt just gone through and everything else like a knife through butter.

When they found her, Honey Belle would have hated to see what the hands sliding over her had done to that beautiful bod.

" 'Brightness falls from the air, / Queens have died young and fair.' " Jury looked up from the theatre program on which Lasko's torch shone and then down at the mutilated body of Honey Belle Farraday.

It was ten-thirty and dark on Wood Street, except for the lights from the torches and the dull blue of the sodium streetlight. The blood, and there was a lot of it, had not had time to congeal. They had to be careful where they stepped.

She had been found by a couple coming from the other end of the block who had been having a late snack in the Golden Egg. The woman had had to be sedated and taken to hospital; her husband had just managed to ring up the police before he got sick all over the telephone kiosk. He was at the Stratford station.

"The doctor says she's been dead about an hour," said Lasko. "We got the call twenty minutes ago. That means she was lying here forty minutes, and no one saw her?"

Jury looked up and down the street. "Nothing open but the Golden Egg, no pubs nearby, no traffic. It's not surprising. Did you check her for prints? The neck? The throat?"

"*What* neck? *What* throat?" said Lasko, peevishly. "Look at her, man."

"I've looked," said Jury. "I was thinking more of under the chin. Which is how she was probably held, chin pulled back. The rest of the stuff came later."

Stuff was probably the right word. After the throat had been slit, laid open back to the cartilage, the torso had been slashed from breastbone nearly to the thigh.

"So there it is again, then," said Lasko, wearily, handing the theatre program back to the Scene of Crimes man.

They watched as the remains of Honey Belle Farraday were placed onto a polyethylene sheet. Jury didn't envy the police photographer. The bright flashes made blurred and misty arcs in the air like tracers and illuminated the night and the white faces of the curious who had gathered at both ends of the street. Police cars, red lights whirring, were stationed at either end and barricades erected. Jury could just see the *Times* and *Telegraph* people racing down the M-1.

"This poem . . . it reminds me of the first one," said Lasko.

"It is the first one. Part of it, I mean." Jury took out the facsimiles of the theatre programs and read:

> "*Beauty is but a flower*
> *That wrinkles will devour;*

Brightness falls from the air,
Queens have died young and fair . . ."

"Where's it from, anyway? Shakespeare?"

Jury shook his head. "I don't know. It sounds familiar, but I don't know." He watched the sheet containing the young girl, shrouded on a stretcher, shoved into the waiting ambulance. He thought of Farraday. The poor bastard. Jury hurt more for the stepfather than for the natural mother. Amelia Blue Farraday, he bet, could be counted on for a royal case of hysterics.

"I'll tell you what worries me," said Jury.

"What?"

"How long is this poem?"

16

Jury had been right about the hysterics.

If there was ever any doubt about Amelia Blue's having been an actress, it was quickly dispelled by her performance over her daughter's murder.

Because that's just what Jury thought it was— a performance. And it was not because he had grown callous in his twenty-odd years with Scotland Yard. After recovering from her initial swoon on the love seat in her Hilton sitting room (or near-swoon: it hadn't put her out of action long), there was a flying at Farraday with fingernails unsheathed, as if she were blaming him for having brought them to this murdering town in the first place; there was a raging at Lasko and Jury, the messengers who had brought the bad news; there was a stalking of the room, as if she'd got the stage blocking down pat. Go to window. Stare out. Move to table. Pick up picture of Honey Belle taken last summer. *Only* last summer, with her pack of boyfriends at the beach. Clasp frame against bosom.

And she had the bosom for clasping. Perhaps the seed of Jury's suspicion of Amelia's maternal feelings had been planted by Penny as they sat by the River Avon.

If Farraday was a self-made man, Jury could see why. His control was far more convincing than the mother's lack of it. Danger, a statue that had suddenly decided to move and speak, had subdued his former anger over the boy's being missing, his loudmouthed demands for more and better police investigation, his threats regarding the American Embassy. His generally throwing his weight around.

It was instead Amelia Blue who had thrown one or two things; it was her husband who had restrained her.

"Hush up, Amelia. It won't do no good, acting this way—"

"*You!* What do—well, maybe *you* just don't *care!* Maybe except only that pore, sweet li'l thing's not around anymore for you to—"

Farraday hit her. Not hard, but a backhanded slap that didn't budge her from where she stood, hands on hips, cheeks flaming. Her brightly rouged lips smiled one of the nastiest smiles Jury had ever seen.

They had all seemed to have forgotten Penny. She had gone outside to sit on a hard little bench in the shadowy darkness of the balcony, as if shadows and darkness were her lot in life. Leaving Lasko to referee and try to question the Farradays, Jury went out to sit beside her.

Penny was staring straight ahead at nothing or at some unspeakable scene being played out in her mind. Her long hair had been done in an awkward, loose braid up on top of her head, and it was spilling down now, the small flower that had been wound in it dead. The hairdo and the shapeless cotton dress at whose folds she was absently plucking Jury assumed had been donned for that night's performance of *Hamlet*, from which she had come back to find this news.

It was odd. It was Penny who really would have made the actress. Her silence was heavy with tragedy, but real tragedy. In her ill-fitting gown and disheveled hair, he half-expected her to say, again, *"Here's rosemary . . . that's for remembrance."*

But she didn't. He felt he must break her silence, for he knew it had a lot to do with guilt, and he put his arm around her.

In a whisper worse than a scream, she finally said, "Where's Jimmy?" And she started to sob, covering her face with her hands, leaning against Jury.

He knew what connection she was making. It was what Jury had been wondering too, ever since they'd found Gwendolyn Bracegirdle. Someone seemed to have it in for the people on Honeysuckle Tours.

Jury pulled her closer and said, "We'll find him; not to worry." How often had he uttered those empty words today?

Penny leaned away from him and wiped her hand indelicately under her nose and down her dress. He pulled out his handkerchief, which she took and held but didn't use, except to twist it in her hands.

"Oh, Gawd! I feel so *guilty*. All them awful things I said about Honey Belle . . . well, but I can't take them back now. And there was times I just *wished* she'd—die."

The stricken glance at Jury told him she knew she'd have to pay for that searing bit of honesty. "The Lord will strike me *dead* for all them things I said." And she looked away, quickly.

Unintentional verse, he thought, like an amateur's attempt to imitate something like the brilliance of that poem which he had just read: *Brightness falls from the air, | Queens have died young and fair.*

Jury increased his hold on Penny Farraday.

And wondered, as she had wondered, where her brother was.

Fifteen minutes later Lasko and the Chief Superintendent were arguing in the lobby of the Hilton, while Jury, smoking a cigarette, looked on.

"Unless we arrest them all—and on the basis of *what* evidence?—I don't see how we can keep the whole damned tour in Stratford if they want to go to London. Except Farraday. He wants to stay here till the kid's found, but with the wife hysterical and wanting to get out . . . I mean, it's not like Stratford-upon-Avon has fond memories for her—"

"She's crazy, then. Either crazy or guilty." Then Sir George, apparently not wanting to neglect Scotland Yard altogether, invited Jury to join the argument. "According to what you told me the other girl said, the woman was jealous as hell of her daughter—"

Lasko tipped back his bowler. "But to do *that* to her own daughter—"

"For God's sake, Sam. What are you going to say next? Blood is thicker than water? Damnit, the people on this tour are *suspects*."

"I just said it: on what evidence do I hold them? How can we say those two women weren't murdered by some Stratford psycho?"

"Some poetry-loving psycho." Sir George snorted. "I'll bet. Have you found out where those four lines of poetry come from?"

"No," said Lasko.

"No? Why not? You waiting for the library to open in the morning?"

"It's not that easy; we don't have any Elizabethan experts on the force—"

Jury interrupted. "You've got one among the suspects."

They both stared at him.

"Schoenberg. He knows a hell of a lot about the period. Assuming it *is* that period. He's writing some sort of book on Christopher Marlowe."

"Which hotel's he at, Sam?"

Lasko checked his list. "Hathaway."

"Go over there and talk to him." Then, morosely, Sir George regarded Jury. "I expect if they must go to London, they must."

Jury looked back, expressionless. He had a feeling that neither Sir George nor Lasko minded all that much.

Wasn't it bad enough, wondered Melrose Plant, that he should be missing out on a murder, without having to sit here in the lobby of the Hathaway Hotel at nearly midnight, listening to Harvey Schoenberg wax anecdotal? Robert Cecil (Bob), son of Lord Burghley; Tom Watson (Tom), friend of Marlowe; Robert Greene (another Bob), friend of Marlowe and enemy of Shakespeare—Harvey Schoenberg had trotted out all the hottest gossip about them over cigars and brandy and he was now into the adventures of Wally Raleigh.

"Are you referring," asked Melrose frostily, "to *Sir Walter* Raleigh?" For some reason, he felt bound to defend the dignity of all of these dead Elizabethans, spies or not. He only wished that Sir Walter Raleigh had been there to see Vivian back to the Hathaway. Sir Walter could, no doubt, have found some remarkably gentlemanly way of extricating himself from the hands of Harvey Schoenberg.

"Sure. You know what he was up to," said Harvey, now comfortably settled in the companion armchair to Plant's.

"Vaguely." Melrose rattled his magazine. "Had something to do with the Babbington Plot against Queen Elizabeth." *Why* was he encouraging this computer programmer to talk?

"No, no, no. *That* was Tom Babbington."

"Well, I *did* deduce that Babbington had something to do with the Babbington Plot." Melrose adjusted his gold-rimmed spectacles and went back to *Country Life,* a magazine he normally loathed. But he had snatched it up from the reading table to hide behind. He leafed quietly through it while Schoenberg filled him in on the details of Sir Walter Raleigh's alleged atheism and passing out of seditious books in his efforts to keep the pot on the boil regarding Mary, Queen of Scots. Melrose looked at horses, looked at houses, looked at hounds, while Harvey told him about Kit Marlowe's barroom brawls, expending rather a lot of energy on the one in Hog Lane. Or ones. Kit always seemed to be fighting. Melrose yawned, and then suddenly grew alert.

Saved. Superintendent Jury was coming through the door of the hotel, saw him sitting here, obviously realized he was in the throes of *taedium vitae*, and quickly came over with the other detective, Lasko.

"Detective Superintendent Richard Jury. Mr. Schoenberg," said Melrose, and watched Harvey's face light up. Someone new.

"Just call me Harve." He grabbed Jury's hand.

"Sure, Harve," said Jury with what struck Melrose as revolting warmth of manner. But that was Jury. "This is Detective Sergeant Lasko."

Harvey shook hands. "I've just been filling Mel in on a few things about Shakespeare. See, I'm a computer—"

"Yes. Mr. Plant told me. What I was chiefly interested in, though, was your expertise when it comes to the Elizabethans."

Scotland Yard calling on Harvey Schoenberg for advice? Melrose wondered if he hadn't landed in the middle of the Mad Hatter's tea party.

Schoenberg, of course, nearly gagged in his willingness to help out. And both of them came near to gagging when Lasko told them the reason.

"My God," said Harvey, looking a little green. "Well . . . but fire away. What do you want to know?"

Lasko repeated the four lines of poetry. "Sound familiar to you?"

But comprehension failed to dawn in Harvey's face as he mouthed them over again. Indeed, he seemed totally vulnerable without his

Ishi. Finally, he shook his head. "Sorry. No comprende."

" 'Brightness falls from the air . . .' That sounds awfully familiar." Melrose said it several times, as if the brightness were indeed drifting down in silver motes.

"That 'Beauty is but a flower'—that's not the first line of a poem. Otherwise, we'd have pegged it by now. But there's no way to index every line of every poem—"

Harvey ran his hands through his hair. "Oh, *God!* If only I had my IBM 8000."

They all looked at him and looked away.

"If it's Shakespeare, Marlowe—either of them—I guarantee I can find it. On the computers I got at home, I could find *anything.*"

Jury only wished that extended to missing boys.

17

Jell-O.

The steps had stopped at the door; the tray had clattered to the floor; the tray-bearer had listened to the groans from within. And then, in true Man-in-the-Iron-Mask fashion, he or she had walked away without so much as investigating the death-rattle. The footsteps had receded, leaving behind only silence and Jell-O.

James Carlton Farraday looked down at the tray and thought at least the gray cat would be happy. This time the small scarlet mold swam in a little lake of milk.

The cat, whose ears had pricked at the sound of the steps, thudded to the floor like a soft pillow, strolled to inspect the lunch. Its lunch, it must by now be thinking. It sniffed the hamburger, nosed the fries, and stepped in the dish of slaw to get to the Jell-O. It curled its tail around its legs and lapped and licked.

As James Carlton sat on the floor and picked up the hamburger, he wondered if a cat could die eating nothing but Jell-O, and then decided this cat had so much fat on it to use up it would live to a hundred if it never ate another bite.

James Carlton was feeling pretty hungry himself. He reasoned that Plan Number Four—Hunger Strike—probably wouldn't work much better than Plan One—for even if he didn't eat the rest, they'd still think he ate the Jell-O. Thus rationalizing Hunger Strike away, he took a look inside his hamburger. Just the way he liked it: ketchup, mustard and two slices of dill pickle.

First he lay down and munched at the hamburger and then he got up and took down the picture and made his entry on the back. The time, the meal. He studied his list and decided it was time to put Plan Number Two into operation.

Having had its lunch and washed itself, the cat clawed its way back up to the bed, where it circled and circled, making its spot to sleep in. It regarded James Carlton lazily, as he started pushing the bureau over under the window. It made a great deal of noise, he thought; yet, no footsteps came down the hall outside in response to it. That was probably because they never came up to the turret except to bring the tray. After positioning the bureau, he pulled out the bottom drawer and the third one up and used those two as stairsteps. The bureau was heavy and he wasn't; otherwise, it would have tilted. The leg up the drawers gave allowed him to pull himself the rest of the way, and he was finally able to peer out the little window by standing on his toes atop the bureau.

What he saw was a curve of water and massed treetops. That must be the Avon over which the river-mist lay. He was not far, then, from Stratford. Viewing was especially difficult because there were narrow bars over the windows. He couldn't see the purpose of them this far above ground. Also, he thought it funny that someone had gone to the trouble of making gauzy curtains. He supposed that it was a Castle Keep he was in, and whoever owned it had decided to give it this homey touch: had got rid of the chains and manacles, cleared out the old bones of other prisoners, and then put in the bureau and pictures and curtains.

The walls were probably too slick for scaling and there was not a branch of a tree near enough for a prisoner to grab hold of and swing down to the ground and to safety. Even if the prisoner could get past the bars. James Carlton looked again at those curtains and then back at the bed, at the sheets and the blanket. If they were all tied together they just might reach down the outside wall.

The gray cat looked back at him, yawned, and then seeing activity that might be deserving of attention in this otherwise dull environment, slid to the floor, scrambled from drawer to drawer and did a perfect three-point landing on top of the bureau.

They both surveyed the mortar around one of the bars. It looked cracked. The sill must have been six inches wide at least. James Carlton tugged at the bar. Loose. A patch of mortar crumbled and rolled off the edge. Quickly, he drew out his pocket knife and went to work, stabbing and jabbing away. Its big paws tucked under its chest, the cat looked on. It seemed to like the operation and started to purr like a train engine. James Carlton's digging away at the bar seemed to make it immensely happy, and he decided the cat might be the reincarnation of some old prisoner who'd died up here and now finally saw a way out. Did it think, he wondered, that it was going to climb down the sheets with him? Fat chance—

Footsteps.

He looked at his watch. Had he really been working at the loose bar until dinnertime? But the cat knew what the steps meant, and bounded down the bureau, collapsing in a heap first, and then padding to the slot in the door.

Cold sweat beaded James Carlton's forehead. But why worry? No one had ever come in before.

The steps paused. The tray clattered down to the floor. The trapdoor opened while the cat crouched before it as if it were a mousehole. The tray was shoved through.

From his bureau perch, James Carlton looked down.

Jell-O.

*   *   *

Back on his bed once again, he licked the chicken grease from his fingers and the cat licked its paws. The window was beginning to purple over with the coming on of the night sky. He could even see two cold stars up there somewhere. He yawned. Might as well leave the bar until morning. But he was bored, and there was nothing around except one recessed bookshelf on which several ancient books rested, long unread in their coverlet of dust. Several of Dickens, dull brown and fox-paged, spotted as if they'd been left out in the rain; a couple of thin volumes of poetry; two cookbooks still wearing their torn jackets.

He unwedged *A Tale of Two Cities;* it was nearly as hard to tug out as the iron bar. James Carlton was a big reader, but he had decided at the outset that he hadn't time for reading, not with all the thinking he'd had to do. He wondered why his captors had been so stupid as to leave books lying around, when they'd gone to the trouble of taking away all the writing paper. If he'd wanted to send a message to someone, he could simply have torn off a page. A person could even code a written text, just by underlining words or letters, and he could do it even without a pencil. That's why he always carried a book of matches: in case someone discovered the pencil stub in his sock. There were lots of things a person could do with matches besides

burning things up. If his captors hadn't knocked
him unconscious, he might have been able to
leave some trail with the matches, although he
imagined they wouldn't have lasted all the way
from Stratford to here.

He looked at the tray and the roll on his plate.
It would be hard by morning, good to crumble,
and if he got lost in the woods he could make a
trail for himself. For he had not the least doubt
he would be in the woods by morning. He took
the roll from the plate.

Hamburgers, chicken, fries—why were his
captors not giving him bread and water to break
down his resistance before they tortured him?
That prospect made him slightly uncomfortable.
But then he reasoned they probably wouldn't,
and that the only reason he had been kidnapped
was for the ransom money. J. C. Farraday was
very rich.

The cat was snoozing away at the foot of the
bed and he felt his own eyes getting heavy.
Going to sleep might prove fatal. He looked
down at Dickens. After all, if you didn't have
enough time to read when you were kidnapped,
when *would* you have time? The binding nearly
cracked when he opened it and the pages crack-
led with age.

Yes, indeed, thought James Carlton. It was
definitely the worst of times. And if it had been
winter, it would certainly have been the winter
of his discontent. Sydney Carton was a pretty

good guy, he thought, stepping in there at the end. His stepfather was always saying how times had changed. It was true. Not many people today, he guessed, would go to the gallows for you. His real father would, of course. And his real mother, too. He looked up from the book and wondered where they were. His father was probably a big-time banker or maybe a ballplayer and looked like Jim Palmer. The Baltimore Orioles was James Carlton's favorite team. He knew who his mother looked like: Sissy Spacek. He knew not so much from that one little picture Penny had, but because Penny herself looked like Sissy Spacek. All those freckles and long hair and the eyes that tilted up just like Sissy. Indeed, although he had never told anyone but Penny, he believed his mother probably *was* Sissy Spacek. He had gone to all of her movies at least three times each. He had forgiven her a long time ago, though; he could understand it must be rough trying to make a go of it in Hollywood, and you could hardly be carting babies around at five o'clock in the morning when you had to get your makeup on. He felt no resentment toward Sissy. After they'd knocked him unconscious, at one point the face of Sissy Spacek had swum before his eyes. It had been very vivid, and very strange. She seemed to be running through bloody streets, bodies and gunfire.

He went back to his book. Old Sydney was

okay, but he'd rather read about Louis being stuffed into that Iron Mask. He closed his eyes and wondered what it would feel like. Would it itch? Over in the wastebasket was a brown paper bag, rolled back as a sort of liner. He pulled it from the wastebasket, studied it a moment, poked two holes above with his pencil and a big hole below and put it over his head and sat down. Of course, he had to imagine that it was hideously weighted and riveted. His face started to itch, but he didn't scratch because if it had been the real thing, he couldn't have. It must have driven poor Louis crazy, like having your arm in a sling for months and months.

Finally, he went ahead and scratched. He put Dickens back and pulled down another book. *The Joy of Cooking.* It looked a hundred years old. James Carlton didn't know a thing about cooking, but for lack of something better to do he looked up chicken. He was amazed to find there were so many things you could do with chicken. He read the recipes through the holes in the paper bag. Chicken and dumplings, Southern Fried, barbecued, chicken with unpronounceable names. He must have had the Southern Fried tonight—

He dropped the book with a thud and stared ahead of him, thinking about that chicken . . . and then about that hamburger. Just the way he liked it . . .

He raced to the bureau and clambered up to

look out at darkness. Not total darkness yet, the massed treetops, some of their leaves showing wet like patent leather with the light from the moon that shone like a bright dollar in the sky. He had been so gripped by fear and excitement, he hadn't realized he was still wearing the bag. He yanked it off and pressed his face against the bars. What he saw was the moon making a streak of silver across the black water—water, trees, bank, all running together in the barest outline of the picture he had seen earlier.

James Carlton had a photographic memory, a faculty which had proved fascinating to people like Harvey Schoenberg and his teachers, but less attractive to people who wished James Carlton would forget some of his more lurid visions. Such as Amelia Blue, who knew that forever fixed in the mind of her stepson were one or two little incidents that would be best forgotten.

Thus he didn't need the light of day to tell him that the river out there was five times as wide as the River Avon.

And he didn't need another taste of the chicken to know it was finger-lickin' good.

Or the hamburger with its spurt of mustard and dab of ketchup and two pickles.

He turned slowly around and stared down at the gray cat. James Carlton, who had gone to some trouble to smooth out that old West Virginia twang from his speech, and who had re-

frained from Penny's *Gawds* and *shits* and other
things that marked one as low-down, now said:
"My gawd, cat. This sure as shit ain't Stratford!"

The gray cat merely opened his eyes a slit,
stretched himself, and went back to his dreams
of mice and Jell-O.

He'd always known it.

18

"London? What do you *mean*, London?" asked Agatha Ardry, helping herself to another toast triangle from Melrose's toast rack. No, she hadn't wanted breakfast, she had said; she'd already eaten with the Randolph Biggets. So he assumed she simply intended to eat his. This was the third piece of toast she was now marmalading. She repeated her question: "Whatever are you going to London for?"

"To look at the Queen," he said, filling in another word in his crossword puzzle.

"And leave me stranded here, I see." Her own moral rectitude intact, she signaled to a waiter and asked for more toast.

"Marooned just like Crusoe, except he only had one Friday, whereas you have many Biggets."

"Well, my dear Plant, for all of your faults, I had at *least* given you credit for being a gentleman. But now I see—" Her peroration upon the loss of Plant's one remaining virtue was interrupted by the waiter's replenishment of the toast rack. "Jury's up to something, isn't he? That's why you're going to London."

Melrose looked up from the crossword. "'Up to something'? Jury is, if you recall, Superintendent of police at New Scotland Yard. I would hardly call an inquiry into another grisly murder on the streets of this otherwise serene town being 'up to something.'"

"Another murder? Another murder?" The toast with its small mountain of quince preserve halted midway to her mouth.

"You don't know? Then you're the only person in Stratford who doesn't. Last night. An American girl from one of the tours. Throat cut ear to ear." He took a perverse delight in delivering this news to her.

Agatha shuddered. "You *are* a ghoul, Plant—"

"I? *I* did not murder the young lady."

"American? American, you say?" Her eyes bulged. "Wasn't that other creature an American, too?"

"Just like you. And the Biggets."

The spoon that had been stirring her third cup of tea clattered to the saucer. "Good lord! Are you suggesting this person has a grudge against Americans?"

"Probably just some old Revolutionary War fanatic."

"Who'd he kill and why?"

"I told you. A young girl, a tourist. I doubt the police know why."

She lowered her voice. "Sex crime, was it?"

"I've no idea." He finished the crossword and thought it must be a new world's record—under fifteen minutes and talking to Agatha at the same time. Melrose prepared to leave and handed her the paper. "Read all about it."

"Where're you going?"

"I told you. To London."

"Well, the Biggets and I certainly shall not stay in Stratford another moment," she said decidedly as she laid down her napkin.

Eyes narrowed, he regarded her. "And where are you going, then?"

"To Long Piddleton, I should think."

Melrose leaned across the table and said in a level voice, "If I return to Ardry End and find even so much as *one* Bigget housed there, I shall personally escort him or her to the Piddle River."

"Well, really! It is such a shame you haven't the hospitality of your dear, dead parents. Your dear mother, Lady Marjorie, the Countess of Caverness—"

He closed his eyes in pain. "Why is it, Agatha, you must always refer to my parents like a butler announcing the entrance of guests to a ball?" He rose and looked down at her. "Remember. *One* Bigget—" and he made a slashing motion beneath his chin.

Rather a grisly gesture, he thought, in the circumstances.

*   *   *

At nine forty-five that morning, Melrose was
the only other reader in the Stratford library in
addition to a palsied old man who slowly
turned the pages of a magazine and coughed
rhythmically. Otherwise, the place was quiet as
a tomb, as Melrose sat writing, a book of Elizabethan poetry open before him.

Since the library had no copy machine, he was
laboriously writing the entire poem out in long-
hand. There were many stanzas. He supposed
he could have approached the librarian about
taking the book out, but he imagined his being a
non-Stratfordian would result in reels of red
tape.

He capped his pen, reread the poem, and
closed the book. The ticking of a longcase clock,
the rustle of the magazine, the occasional tap-
ping of the librarian's heels were the only
sounds, as he sat thinking over the events of the
last twenty-four hours. He then rose, reshelved
the book of poetry, went to the card catalogue,
returned with a number to another shelf and
took down another book.

This he sat reading for an hour. Then he
closed that book also. His fingers drummed on
the cover as he thought about it.

A minor point, perhaps (thought Melrose,
frowning), but strange, nonetheless.

19

When Jenny Kennington opened the door of the narrow little house in Ryland Street in the old part of Stratford, Jury felt a small jolt, not because she had changed but because she hadn't. Not only the same hair, but worn in the same way, pulled back and carelessly tied at the base of her neck by a small headscarf, the oak-colored ends curling up. It might not have been the same skirt—all good wool looked the same—but it was certainly the same sweater. He remembered how its silvery thread had caught the late sun as they stood in the great empty dining room of Stonington.

"Superintendent Jury!" The smile came quickly and was as quickly erased, as if she wasn't sure what her position with him was. But after her initial surprise, as she stepped aside to admit him, she seemed aware of a secret that neither of them knew they'd shared.

Jury found himself staring at a familiar scene: the room—a front parlor of sorts—was full of packing boxes, some full and strapped, others half-full or empty. She was not, he knew, moving in.

She followed the direction of his gaze and raised her arms and let them drop again in a gesture of helplessness. Her expression was not happy as she said, "I never seem to be able to offer you a chair. The furniture, except for a bed and a few other things, I've sold already. Well, there didn't seem much sense in moving all of those bulky things . . ."

"The chair doesn't matter. Is this sturdy enough to sit on?" He indicated one of the strapped boxes.

"Yes, of course."

Gingerly, he sat on the edge of the packing case.

She sat down too, on the one facing him. "Do you have a cigarette?"

"Of course." He brought out a pack. There was only one left. When he saw her reach and then hesitate, he said, "Go on, take it. I'm trying to cut down anyway." He would have given a month's pay for a cigarette and a bottle of whiskey at that moment to get him through this. Still she hesitated. "Go on," he urged.

"We'll share it."

"Okay," he said, smiling, and lighting it for her. "Where're you going?"

"There's an aunt of mine, elderly and rather ill. She wants to go on a sea voyage and needs someone to go with her. I'm the only family she's got left. And she's all of mine. The rest are dead." She exhaled and passed the cigarette to Jury. "It's funny. Other people seem to keep adding to their lives—you know, husbands, children, grandchildren—; I seem to keep diminishing."

There was no self-pity in the words, which were more highly charged simply because she said them so flatly.

Jury took a drag on the cigarette, tasting her mouth like a memory, and handed it back. "It doesn't have to be that way."

Her gaze seemed fixed on a point in air over his shoulder. "I wonder." Her eyes rested on his, then.

He tried on a smile; it didn't seem to work very well. "If it's just a voyage you're going on—" He looked around the room. "Then why all this?"

"It's going to be a long voyage, I'm afraid."

The cigarette she had handed back to him was nearly spent. He did not smoke it. He was afraid of its going out. "But when you get back . . . I mean, you've got to settle somewhere. Don't you know where?"

Shaking her head, she said, "Not really. It might be that I'll live with Aunt Jane for a while. Though, really, I don't think she's got that long in her condition—"

"You don't have to go," he said suddenly.

"I wish you'd come before," she said.

Jury watched the ash inch microscopically down the white cylinder and remembered the last time he'd seen her. Dust and ashes seemed to come between them. He wondered if he were growing fatalistic. "You can't just drift about for the rest of your life."

"We used to live—my family, I mean—here. Not in Stratford. A ways outside of it. The place was much too large just for me to come back to. Anyway, it's completely run down now, the wings are mostly rubble; the gate house is a sort of mound—"

It was as though she were picking up the thread of a conversation after an interruption of minutes rather than months.

". . . When I went out there I realized you can't get the past back again."

"'Of course you can.'" The cigarette was burning his fingers. He had to let it drop on the bare floor. She put her foot over it, ground it out.

When he looked up at her she was smiling bleakly. "I've never heard anyone say that. Do you really believe it?"

"It was Gatsby who said it. You know. Fitzgerald's Gatsby. About Daisy."

She seemed to be looking everywhere in the room except at him. "Daisy. Yes."

Jury stood up. "I've got to be going. I'm going to London inside of an hour. Look. You'll still be here, won't you, for a few days? Or could you call me before you leave?" He gave her one of his cards, writing his home number on the back.

"I'll be here for another week, I expect." She looked down at the card. "And yes, I'll call."

At the door, she said sadly, "But it didn't work for him, did it? Gatsby, I mean."

Jury smiled. "I guess it depends how you read it."

As he walked back down Ryland Street, he realized that not once had the subject of murder come up between them.

20

Having had Agatha for breakfast, Melrose was now having Harvey Schoenberg for lunch. There he sat, his arm draped over his computer, drinking stout, when Melrose entered the Dirty Duck fifteen minutes later.

"Hey, Mel!" he called above the voices of a rather thinner lunch-crowd than usual. The tourists must have scattered like buckshot following the discoveries of the last two days.

"Good morning," said Melrose, depositing his stick on the table. "I thought Honeysuckle Tours would be on its way to London by now."

"It's J.C. that's holding us up. You know, Farraday. Your friend Rick's trying to talk him into going. Says he won't budge—"

" 'Rick'?"

"Yeah. The Scotland Yard guy." Harvey raised his glass. "Want one?"

"Sherry, if you don't mind. Tio Pepe, dry."

"Tio. Got it. Guard this, okay?" he nodded to the Ishi computer.

"With my life."

Harvey went off to the bar and Melrose drew the folded sheet of paper from his pocket. He reread it, especially the stanza the murderer had appropriated for his own macabre use.

A few minutes later, Harvey was back, putting down the sherry and picking up the conversation as if he hadn't been gone. "After all, you can hardly blame the poor bastard, since Jimmy hasn't come back yet." He lowered his voice. "You don't think something's happened to the kid, do you?" When Melrose didn't answer immediately, he nudged him. "You know what I mean."

"I know. But it doesn't quite fit the pattern, does it?"

"Pattern? What pattern?"

"Both victims have been women. You knew the Farraday boy pretty well, didn't you? That is, he talked to you more than anyone else on the tour."

"Could be. About computers. I never saw anyone catch on so quick to computers. I was trying to set his sights toward the future. You know—career-wise. Kid's a real brain. Well, I better be going." He drained his glass, stood up, and slung the strap of the case over his arm. "Man, I can hardly wait to get to London. Can you feature it? Deptford, that's the first place I'm hitting. Southwark, and maybe Greenwich. Listen, you should let me show you around." He held out his hand, palm up, and tapped it. "I know the other side of the Thames like the palm of my hand, at least the way it was. It's all those maps I read. Of course, I guess it's different now." He sighed, and was off, managing to raise some indignant eyebrows as the computer hammered at a few elbows on the way out.

Jury was just coming in as Schoenberg was going out. They exchanged a few words and Harvey nodded, cuffed Jury on the shoulder, and went on.

"Hello, Rick," said Melrose, pushing out a chair. "Sit down and take the weight off."

"Thanks. Honeysuckle Tours is booked into Brown's Hotel. Let's hope they stay put."

"I can guarantee Harvey won't. He's got a brother coming to London, for one thing; not that I think brother Jonathan will be much of a companion in Harvey's rambles. He's already wandering mentally all over Southwark and Deptford. He has invited me along."

"He told me. About the brother, I mean. Apparently stays at Brown's, too, when he's in town. Honeycutt wasn't kidding about his little group. The check we've run on them certainly shows they're none of them hurting for cash." Jury sighed. "No way to stop them leaving their hotel. Amelia Farraday's ready to take the first plane back to the States; I'm not sure whether it's to put distance between her and bad memories or between her and the Metropolitan Police. But I imagine we can find some way to block *that* move. Are you ready to leave? I'm having a drink first and something to eat. Incidentally, I got you digs at Brown's, too. You can keep an eye on them. Let Harvey show you round Southwark. What the hell's he expect to find?"

"The inn where old Kit Marlowe was killed raise its ghostly rafters over the Thames, I expect. I've done your homework for you. The poem—I wrote it down."

As Melrose took some legal-length foolscap from his pocket, Jury said, "How the hell did you find it when we've had every man in the department scouring books of poetry—?"

"Simple. I assumed it was Elizabethan and fairly well anthologized and just got the fattest collection I could lay hands on in the library. I looked in the index of first lines."

"But I thought we said it wasn't a first line."

"It isn't. I used metrics." Melrose adjusted his gold-rimmed spectacles. "I eliminated at least three-fourths of the poems in the book that way. Perhaps more. It's very regular rhythm, and it's *also* iambic trimeter. Had it been pentameter, or something, it would have been harder. I just ticked off every first line in trimeter."

"Hell," said Jury, smiling.

"Yes. Irritatingly clever of me, wasn't it?" He cleared his throat and read:

> *"Beauty is but a flower*
> *Which wrinkles will devour;*

Brightness falls from the air,
Queens have died young and fair;
Dust—"

At that moment, the door to the Dirty Duck opened. *Oh, God!* Melrose thought. He had forgotten completely about Vivian Rivington, and there she stood.

He shoved the papers in Jury's face. "Here, read it."

"For Christ's sakes, I'm not blind!" Jury said, lowering the paper and his head with it.

They were sitting back in a corner. It was quite possible she would move on with her companion—a slim, dark fellow, no doubt the fiancé. Wonderful. Now, if only she didn't turn and look around the room—

She turned.

And, of course, just then Jury, having read through the poem, raised his head to say something to Melrose.

He was glad he wasn't standing in the way of the look that shot between Vivian and Jury.

"I'll be damned—" Jury muttered, rising as she started toward their table, smiling and looking wonderful in nothing but jeans and a white silk blouse, the dark man in tow.

She held out her hand. "Inspector Jury, for heaven's sakes—"

"Miss Rivington. This is certainly a surprise."
How   banal,   thought   Melrose,   relieved

nonetheless. If they had never got beyond *Inspector* and *Miss*, what the hell was he worried about? Or was all this formality and everyone's not knowing what to do with their hands or say next merely for the sake of the Count of Monte Cristo behind her?

"I'm sorry, I—" Vivian turned to the swarthy fellow with the aquiline face, who stood with European gravity, hands in pockets of blazer, thumbs out, bending politely toward them. "Franco Giapinno, my, ah—Inspector Richard Jury and Lord—I mean, and Melrose Plant."

She blushed, the old familiar Vivian, like a child who'd forgotten lines in a play. There were murmurs of *pleased-to-meet-you* and small, guttural Italian utterances from Vivian and Giapinno, to whom Melrose took an immediate dislike.

"Why is it a surprise?" asked Vivian of Jury. "Didn't Melrose tell you I was here—?"

Her voice trailed off as Jury leveled a look at Melrose that would have stopped a stampede of buffalo.

"No," was all he said.

Melrose felt wedged between their looks. "Well, it isn't 'Inspector,' anyway, Vivian," he said heartily. "It's 'Superintendent' now."

"It certainly should be," she said with that sincerity that had always made even her most banal comments glow. "Franco and I, ah, are . . ."

Where she dropped it, Franco seemed only too happy to pick it up. "Engaged." With a disgustingly proprietorial gesture, Franco put his arm round her waist.

Everybody smiled.

Jury refused Giapinno's invitation to join them for luncheon. "Sorry, but I'm just on my way to London. The car's outside."

"Oh," said Vivian, weighing the syllable with sadness. "It's about . . . I heard there'd been a murder in Stratford . . . Is that it—?"

"That's it," said Jury, rather overcrisply.

The silly good-byes were like the silly hellos. Vivian and the Italian moved off. At least, thought Melrose, there hadn't been an invitation to the wedding.

There was a long silence as the two of them stood there. Melrose studied the floorboards, almost afraid to look at Jury, who was fumbling through the lighting of a cigarette.

Jury finally spoke through a haze of smoke rising upwards.

"Of all the gin joints in all the towns in all the world—she had to walk into mine."

II

DEPTFORD

*"It strikes a man as dead
As a great reckoning in a little room."*

—*As You Like It*

21

Detective Chief Superintendent Racer slapped shut the folder and glared across his desk at Detective Sergeant Alfred Wiggins, who, being totally innocent of any prior involvement with this case, was therefore the most likely target for Racer's acrimony.

Wiggins did what he always did in difficult circumstances—blew his nose.

"Sorry to drag you out of sickbay, Sergeant," said Racer with mock-solicitousness.

With Wiggins, the sarcasm fell wide. Jury sat there thinking that Wiggins's long survival was owing to his ability to take everything literally. "Quite all right, sir. It's just this allergy. The pollen count this week has been fearful—"

Racer's face, already spongy-red from too many brandies for lunch at his club, grew redder with suppressed rage. Not suppressed for long, however. "I don't give a bloody damn about the pollen count. I'm not a bee. And put that damned packet away!"

Some men went for their guns under stress,

some for their cigarettes. Wiggins went for his cough drops. He had just been stripping the cellophane from a fresh box. "Sorry, sir."

Jury yawned and continued to look out of the window of Racer's office at the sludgy gray sky above New Scotland Yard, at the small square of the Thames beyond the embankment. Racer insisted on a room with a view. All the better, thought Jury, if he decided to throw himself out the window some day. Racer's voice droned on at Wiggins, and Jury waited. He knew the Chief Superintendent was merely prepping for the real operation of dissecting Jury: pulling on the rubber gloves, lining up the knives, the scalpels, the forceps. Racer had missed his true calling with the Met. He should have been a medical examiner.

Having finished with Wiggins, who looked a bit pale (but then, Wiggins always did), Racer rocked back in his leather swivel chair, picked a bit of lint from his exquisitely tailored suit, adjusted the miniature carnation in his buttonhole, and turned his thin-bladed smile on Jury.

"The Slasher," he said, looking at Jury as if The Slasher sat before him in all of his bloody glory. "It's really remarkable, *Superintendent*," (Racer had never forgiven Jury his promotion last year) "that you happen to go to Stratford-upon-Avon and manage to come back with two murders and one missing person to your credit." Jury might have been a collector, the way Racer put it. He rose from his chair to take his usual few turns about the room and added magnanimously, "*Not* that I can hold you personally responsible for this lunatic's activities—"

"Thank you," said Jury.

A pause. "*Superintendent* Jury, sarcasm is both unprofessional and unprofitable." He stood behind them, feeling perhaps a psychological advantage in talking to the backs of their heads. Wiggins, Jury noted out of the corner of his eye, took the opportunity to open his box of cough drops very quietly.

"However," Racer went on, "it's not enough, is it, that you insist on *involving* yourself in a case that rightly belongs to the Warwickshire constabulary—did *they* ask for assistance from us? No indeed, they did not! Leaving *me* to smooth over things and soft-soap the Chief Constable—"

Soft-soap? Racer? A bowl of acid in the eyes would be more like it. Padding behind them, a tiger without teeth, Racer droned on.

Metaphorically in his death throes, Chief Superintendent Racer still refused to die. Jury's colleagues at New Scotland Yard had all been looking forward to Racer's retirement last year. But it hadn't occurred; Racer was still slouching toward it as if it were terminal. Having been so sure the Chief Superintendent was on his way out, they had rallied round the coffin (again,

metaphorically speaking) only to find the corpse
had scarpered and been resuscitated at its desk
on Monday, Savile Row trousers knife-creased,
buttonhole boutonniered.

"—not enough, oh, no! *Then* instead of quietly
leaving it all to the Stratford boys, you *bring the
whole lot to London!* Why, Jury? To *London!* To
London!—"

"To buy a fresh pig," Jury couldn't help himself sometimes.

Silence. The padding stopped. Wiggins shot
Jury a glance and then stared straight ahead,
sucking stealthily on his cough drop.

Leaning over Jury's shoulder, breathing the
effluvium of his brandy-and-sodas into Jury's
face, Racer said, "What was that, lad?"

"Nothing, Sir."

The padding resumed. "Ever since you made
superintendent, Jury—"

Jury wished he'd kept his mouth shut. Now
he'd deflected the lecture into even saltier
streams of vituperation, for now Racer could get
on Jury's roller-coaster career. "You got *up*, lad.
You can just as easily go *down*. . . ."

Hell, at this rate they'd be here all afternoon.

Fortunately, Racer's secretary interrupted by
walking in and dumping some papers on his
desk. Fiona Clingmore was dressed today in
what should have been a negligee, but was apparently a summer dress. It was black and lay-

ered with ruffles all down the front, the layers
being the only thing that kept Fiona from absolutely showing through. She stood now, one
hand leaning on the desk, the other on her out-
slung hip, scarlet fingernails drumming, and
giving them all the benefit of her décolletage.
Fiona had topped forty a couple of years ago,
Jury knew, but she was going down fighting.

"*Miss* Clingmore," said Racer, "I would appreciate your knocking, if you don't mind. And
get that mangy cat out of here."

"Sorry," she said, wetting her finger and re-
plastering a curl against her cheek. "You're to
sign these straightaway. The A.C. wants them."
She flounced out, forgetting the cat, but not forgetting to give Jury a wink. He was fond of
Fiona and her increasingly bravura perfor-
mances. He winked back.

The cat snaked its way round their several
legs and immediately leapt to Racer's desk,
where it sat, solid as a paperweight.

Racer shoved it off, uttering expletives that
cats were apparently privy to, and sat down.
"Now what the hell's this group you've got
staying at Brown's? Are they implicated?"

"I don't know," said Jury. "I only know that
the two who were murdered in Stratford and the
missing boy were all on this same tour."

Racer snorted. "And did you tell the press
that, Jury? They've been running up and down
the M-40 like lemmings."

"I don't talk to the press. I leave that to you."

"Well, *somebody* damn well talked! Probably those bloody swedes in Stratford."

Jury shifted impatiently in his chair, reaching down to pet the cat, who apparently shared their feelings about Racer. "I think it would be best if Sergeant Wiggins and I were permitted to get on with it before there's another murder," he said calmly.

"Another murder? What do you mean by that?"

"That the murderer isn't through yet. The message hasn't been fully delivered."

Racer's eyebrows knotted. "Explain that, will you?"

"Well, you've seen those lines of poetry. Two lines left with the Bracegirdle woman's body; two with the Farraday girl's. In that one stanza he's got three lines to go." And to send Racer's blood pressure up a bit, Jury added, "Then he can start a new stanza, of course."

The idea of a string of murders as long as a string of pearls or a twelve-stanza poem apparently could even make Racer see reason.

"You think there's going to be another murder." He looked from Jury to Wiggins and back again. "Then why the hell are you two sitting here wasting my time? Get the lead out."

22

Thought I didn't know what she was doing, didn't she? Amelia Blue Farraday stood outside one of Soho's more popular strip joints, looking at the life-sized posters. *It's where she'd of wound up, place like this,* thought Amelia, looking perhaps longer than she actually needed to in order to placate the devils of lust and degradation walking the streets—

"'Ello, love."

"Just lookin'?"

The questions came from a lanky fellow with slicked-back hair and his chunky friend standing next to him cracking his knuckles. "Show you a good time, we could."

Amelia looked them over. Back in Georgia you stepped on this kind when it slithered across your shoe. Amelia did not bother to answer. Nor did she bother to try and walk around them; that would be like giving place. She simply reached out, pushed the two apart, and walked on down Soho Street.

Just as well she's dead, thought Amelia. *Just as*

*well. She'd've let those two crumbs take her for all
she was worth.* And with that unrepentant and
unremorseful thought, Amelia stopped before
another giant hoarding outside a cheap movie
house. *I'd of seen her plastered on posters all up
and down Second Avenue. Good God, that child
would stop at nothing. . . .*

Bored with lemonade and beer on the veranda, bored with James C.'s clumsy lovemak-
ing, Amelia had taken up with what she called
"casuals"—just the first man who came along.
But she'd done it for *pleasure*, not *money*—
though of course there'd been the little gift here
and there—not like Honey Belle, out there *selling* herself, no better'n a common whore.
Honey Belle'd turned out just like her old man,
that no-good, two-timing bastard that thought
he was God's gift.

The seedy-looking crowd flowed around her
as she did her drumroll walk on through Soho,
and she knew some of the jostling wasn't acci-
dental. She tossed her yellow hair—she still
wore it long, no matter that little runt of a beau-
tician told her, Sweetie, it adds years to you.
Her hair'd always been white-blond and her
crowning glory. No little London fag hair-
dresser was going to fool with it. Toss it up on
top of her head and put combs in it and she
looked like a queen.

Amelia was bored with the strip joints and
the blue-movie houses and the cheap Chink

restaurants. It was just that she was damned if she'd sit through even one more play with those fools on Honeysuckle Tours and equally damned if she'd be chained to her room at that snooty hotel. White gloves and bowing and scraping. She was glad James C. had money but she was no snob. Glad he had money, but oh, the dear lord, if only he hadn't got those two kids. Not even *his* kids, that's what Amelia couldn't understand. Vaguely, she wondered where the boy had gone off to. Wished he'd stay away. She knew they both hated her guts but she could care less. She had James C. and the money and if they thought they could do her out of that, they were crazy. . . .

It looked like a whole wall of males walking toward her now—four of them, leering already, even before they got a good look. One big collective leer, and an assortment of obscenities, uttered in that guttural Cockney or whatever it was, that made them swallow their syllables (". . . look a' the knobs o' tha' 'un, Jake . . . Ooooo . . ."). They hardly had the time to get even this much out before Amelia's bosom plowed right through them, with a little help from an elbow in the ribs. She didn't bother to look back when the tone of the remarks changed; she was used to it. The whole exchange barely registered; she went on with her interior monologue regarding Honey Belle. . . .

When that awful little man who claimed he

was a detective had tried to blackmail her, Amelia had paid him off, read the report on Honey Belle, and burned it. She never did know who put the man on the girl's trail, but God help her if James C. ever got wind of what that girl was up to: dirty pictures, dirty movies, the works. Though James C. hadn't much room to talk, that was for sure: not after she'd caught him nearly with his pants down, and Honey Belle right there in the bedroom. Alley cat, that's what the girl was. All her daddy's fault; she was—had been—just like him.

Amelia wasn't looking for action in Soho; she just felt like slumming for a bit before going to meet George. A private club off Berkeley Square. That sounded more like her class of place, from the little she knew of the different London areas. Near the hotel.

Tired of walking, she hailed a cab, collapsed into the seat and tossed her shoes off. God, but walking in this city was hard on the arches. She massaged her feet. He let her out on the square, grumbled at her tip—*Up yours, fella*—and sped off into the night.

Christ, no manners, these Brits. Think just because you're American you can pick it off trees. . . .

Amelia started across the square, humming. Of course it was before *her* time, but hadn't there been an old song about a nightingale singing in Berkeley Square? Must've been First

World War. Didn't her pa used to sing it, sometimes? Amelia heard bird-twitter and stopped to look up at the inky lace of the trees. On a bench by the walk, a drunk snored, huddled under his coat as if it were January instead of July. It had been a long time since she'd thought of her folks, thought of Pa. He was up in heaven somewhere, sleeping it off, like the drunk back there. Nothing but itinerant farmhands they'd been, though of course she'd made up a more suitable background when she'd met James C. Had to hand it to him, though; he wasn't a snob. But even James C. might stick at marrying what a lot of folks still called white trash. Amelia's chin went up. You had to survive in this world. And you had to have some fun while doing it. She swung along, the huge bag she'd got in Nassau last year slung over her shoulder. Fun was what life was all about, wasn't it? Was it her fault if she couldn't feel sadder over Honey Belle's death? It was the hand of Fate, that's all. You die like you live, that's all. So some sex maniac got loose in that twirpy little town and happened to pick on two females from the same tour— Amelia's skin went a little clammy. If her husband, if James C. had happened to find out about Honey Belle, or for that matter *Amelia*— that was ridiculous. She walked on, more slowly. Still, how did she know she could trust that detective not to go to him and offer to sell

the information? *As a matter of fact,* she thought,
*how do I know James C. didn't hire that man? . . .
and maybe did the same to me?* Once again, she
stopped dead in her tracks. She took herself
firmly in hand: *Amelia Blue Farraday, you just got
chiggers up your li'l ol' ass, honey.* Ridiculous.
Her life force once more restored and flowing,
she resumed her stroll through Berkeley
Square.

Or started to. The square was deathly still,
there was no one else out taking the air this
night, and that birdsong halted, started, halted
again, almost as if it were noting her progress.

The arm that suddenly came round her
throat and dragged her neck back was clothed
in old wool. Before she felt something bite into
her neck, she had time for one vagrant thought:
You die like you live.

A small clutch of police officers stood in
Berkeley Square.

Access to the park was cut off by barricades
at the entrances and police constables directing
the foot traffic. Told to move it along, passersby
naturally stayed. Within ten minutes, a neck-
lace of the curious surrounded the square. In
another fifteen minutes, they were six deep.
Motorists were driving by slowly enough to
create a hell of a snarl; many were parking and
getting out to rubberneck. Within twenty minutes after the police arrived, it looked as if half

of London had descended upon Berkeley Square.

Jury looked down at the red pantsuit that had once been white. A proper job The Slasher had done of her, he thought. There wasn't much left that was recognizable except for that mop of pale yellow hair, which had, amazingly enough, escaped soaking, perhaps because of the slant of the head after the throat had been cut. The grass around was rusty-brown and still tacky. A long vertical slash ran from shoulder blade down the length of the torso exposing the stomach wall and organs.

Wiggins looked at Jury. "Same as the ones in Stratford, sir?"

Jury nodded. To the Scene of Crimes officer he said, "What have you found so far?"

The man turned to Jury, looking at him over the top of his notebook. "Guts," he said calmly. He looked almost spiffy in a well-tailored, appropriately funereal dark suit.

"I can see that. The blood must have gone everywhere—"

The Scenes of Crimes man nodded. "Including all over the killer." He nodded over his shoulder. "We found an old coat in the dustbin over there."

"Anything else? Some sort of message, maybe?"

"Good guessing, Superintendent. There was

part of a theatre program. *As You Like It.* Give
me a moment and you and the doc can have the
lot." He finished up his note-taking and the
photographer his pictures.

The pathologist was kneeling beside the
body; he handed up a page torn from the front
of the program, blood-smeared.

"What is it?" asked Wiggins.

Jury read the single line: " *'Dust hath closed
Helen's eye.'* "

"Is it the end of that poem?" asked Wiggins.

"No. There are two more lines."

Farraday managed to stand on his feet when
Jury told him. He reminded Jury of a cliff's
edge eroded again and again by an onslaught
of seawater. One wondered when it would
crumble. Not yet, apparently.

Penny Farraday walked backward into the
shadows and then turned and ran to the bath-
room. Jury could hear the sounds of retching.
He wished he could help her; he was too busy
trying to deal with Farraday.

Farraday, his face as drained as if a knife had
let his own blood, managed to bring the brandy
snifter Jury had handed him up to his lips. His
hand was shaking violently. His mouth worked
a little; he finally said, "When did it happen?"

"The doctor says last night, early this morning. Sometime about midnight, probably."

"Why'd it take so long—?" The voice sounded strangled.

Jury finished the question for him. "So long for the body to be found? Whoever did it hid the body pretty well, under a clump of shrubbery. It was a woman out walking her two dogs who found her. She wouldn't have, except the dogs were snuffling the bushes. We didn't get there until nearly ten this morning."

Farraday seemed to have lost interest in the explanation halfway through. He ran his hand down over his face like a man whose eyes had been hurt from staring too long into the sun.

Jury disliked thinking that if Farraday were putting on an act, it was a damned convincing one. Whoever was doing this was certainly narrowing the suspects. A grim thought. But who else could it be except someone in this tour group? Unless it was a person completely unknown to Jury who had followed Honeysuckle Tours.

"Do you think you can talk about it? Or do you want me to come back?"

In answer, Farraday turned his head, looking back to the doorway through which Penny had gone. "How's Penny?"

"I'll get her, if you want—"

"No, no. Listen. You might as well know it, you'd find it out anyway. Things between me and Amelia, they weren't all that hot."

Meaning absolutely rotten. He refilled the

brandy glass from an assortment of bottles on the table beside the couch and handed it to Farraday.

"Thanks." He drank some more and a little blood suffused his gray face. "I wanted her to stay in last night. Go to dinner with me, Simpson's maybe, and then just stay in. But she wouldn't." He cleared his throat.

"Why?"

"Amelia don't like just to sit around . . ." His voice trailed off.

Jury didn't want to say what he was thinking: *Not even after the murder of her own daughter?*

Farraday said it for him. "My God, wouldn't you'd've thought that after Honey Belle—?" He shook his head and whispered it: "As God is my witness, I don't think she gave much of a damn. Oh, I *know* it don't—didn't—bother her that Jimmy's missing. She never made no bones about him and Penny, the way she felt about them. But Honey Belle—that's her *own flesh*. I don't know, I just don't know."

"Do you think she had a more particular reason for wanting to go out than plain boredom?"

Farraday looked up at him. "A man, you mean?"

Unhappily, Jury nodded.

*   *   *

"Mr. Plant?" said the young woman at Brown's reception desk. "I believe he went out with the gentleman in—" Her eyes drifted so imperceptibly over the cards that Jury had the feeling they never left his face. "—Room 106. Mr. Schoenberg." She smiled. She was a very pretty woman.

"What time did they leave, do you know?" Jury returned the smile.

"Well, I'd say somewhere near nine o'clock."

Jury wished that all of the staff at Brown's could pinpoint the comings and goings of its clientele with such accuracy. "You may have heard. There's been an unfortunate—accident—"

That she had heard was clear from the brief nod, the more sober arrangement of features. A remarkably well-trained staff, thought Jury. Whatever their private amazements, excitements, or thrills, they'd keep themselves to themselves. "This Mrs. Farraday left the hotel last night, latish. Were you here?"

The young woman shook her head, perhaps more saddened that she hadn't been there to supply the Superintendent with more information than by the thought of a guest's untimely demise. "That would have been the night receptionist—" She made as if to pick up the telephone. "—Would you like me to call her?"

Jury shook his head. "Just ask her to call me if she remembers anything about Mrs. Farraday." He dropped a card on the desk. "This Mr. Schoenberg. Harvey. Do you have a booking for his brother?"

Again the discreet eyes flicked through some cards. "We do, yes. There's a Mr. Jonathan Schoenberg expected this afternoon." The light green eyes regarded him hopefully, as if she had finally given up some information he could use.

"Thanks. You've been most kind." Jury smiled again.

The eyes became slightly less discreet.

23

A trip through history with Harvey L. Schoenberg was like following a horse with blinders on. The horse could see everything straight ahead, and as long as it did not have to interpret its position by putting it in the context of views to the left and right, it did its job. Indeed, it did wonderfully well—knew every cobble in the street, every turn of the road, every lamppost.

"Traitors' Gate," said Harvey, rapturously, still talking about the view they had had of it, looking across the massive arches of Tower Bridge. They were now standing on the Southwark side of the River Thames, having been deposited, at Harvey's insistence, right on the other end of the new London Bridge. "Imagine the heads that were stuck up there!"

"If it's all the same to you, I'd sooner not. Public executions and the like never appealed to me. Neither did bear-baiting."

"Oh, come on, Mel! Where's your sense of history?"

"In my stomach."

But Harvey refused to allow any dampening of the spirit, although he was not averse to a dampening of thirst. "Let's find a pub. Right here, nearly where we're standing, was the Bear Tavern, a very popular place." Harvey had faced round, and was pointing off. "Over there was Tooley Street—"

"Over there is still Tooley Street, unless my eyes deceive me."

"Yeah, yeah, but I'm trying to tell you how it *was*, back when Marlowe walked these streets. There were a bunch of pubs up this way—"

"I'm sure there still are."

"—There was even a Black Swan here; north of St. Thomas's Hospital—"

"There is always a Black Swan. There are Black Swans the entire length and breadth of the British Isles."

Harvey sighed and folded the old map of Southwark he'd been consulting. They commenced walking up Southwark Street. Harvey shook his head, a man who cannot understand other men. "You're just not into the spirit of this little pilgrimmage, Mel."

"I thought we were going to Deptford. To Mistress Bull's tavern, where this iniquitous murder took place."

"We are, we are. But we've got to have a walk around Southwark. Think of all the time Marlowe spent here." They had walked down a flight of stone steps and now stood looking up at the imposing facade of Southwark Cathedral. Schoenberg consulted his map, hitching the Ishi farther up on his shoulder. "This was the Church of St. Mary Overies. You know that story? Real sad. Over there was the Stews."

"Stews?"

"Red light district. Southwark was a real cesspool. Criminals used to run over here from the City so they wouldn't be prosecuted—kind of like someone in the U.S. running from one state to another. I wonder where Hog Lane is. That's the place where Kit had the duel with Bill Bradley."

"Marlowe was always having duels. That's why I can't understand your tenacious belief in this absurd theory. Let's have a drink."

They had walked through a series of mean little streets fronting warehouses behind the cathedral until they had come upon a pub, crowded despite its location. Melrose wondered where in heaven's name all of these people came from.

"Look at it this way," said Harvey, clasping his pint of stout between both hands, and looking with earnest gray eyes at Melrose. "Okay, I agree he was always jumping the gun with people. But explain how in the hell could an 'accident' like that happen? I mean, him running his own dagger into his own eye. Or right above it, I mean?"

Melrose lit his cigar. "Simple. Allow me to

demonstrate." Melrose picked up his walking stick. "Assume that the knob of this stick is the hilt of a dagger. Assume you—Frizer—are sitting wedged between Poley and Skeres and Marlowe is pommeling you about the head with the dagger's hilt. It was common to do that in that day and age, a kind of precursor to the serious bit of dueling or whatever. That means that the blade of the knife is pointed *at* Marlowe, doesn't it? So when Frizer is trying to deflect the weapon it goes into Marlowe's forehead." Melrose shrugged. "I don't see why that's so hard to understand."

Harvey looked at him with some respect. "Say, you've really done your homework, haven't you?"

"Yes. I did a little reading in the Stratford library. Somehow I feel it is incumbent upon me to disabuse you of this theory about Shakespeare . . . I mean, *really* . . . oh, not that damned computer again, Harvey, for God's sakes."

But Harvey had the computer out and was punching keys to beat the band. Then he sat, lips pursed, waiting for his file to come up. "Here it is: medical report. A wound like that couldn't have killed him. It would have sent him into a coma."

"Medical report? What medical report?"

Harvey scratched his head. "Well, an interpretation, let's say. By a scholar. And another thing: if all this was going on, why the hell didn't Bob Poley and Nick Skeres *help old Kit out?* Answer me that. They were his buddies, weren't they? So they just sit there? The only reason they'd just sit there is because the *whole thing was planned out in the first place!*" He flicked off the Ishi and raised his glass in a gesture of triumph and gazed around the smoke-filled, crowded room. "Just imagine what these places used to be like."

Melrose hoped whatever imagining was going to take place would be in Harvey's memory bank and not in the Ishi's. If he was forced to watch him bring up one more file, Melrose would seriously consider throwing himself into the Thames.

"Imagine pulling up your horse in the courtyard and having the servants run out to you, the hostler take your horse and the drawer light a fire in your chamber—"

"And the hostler always managing somehow to feel the weight of your purse, and the chamberlain rob you of it afterwards—"

"What a cynic." Harvey continued, in a weepy tone: "And the host helping you off with your boots, just as if it were your own home; and the tapster chalking up the score at the bar—"

"And ye merry host being as much moneylender, guller of country bumpkins and young gallants, as he was publican; and the drawer always managing to add a few more chalk-marks to the board than were rightfully yours—"

"You're really fun, Mel, you know that? But think of the meals you could get, sitting before the blazing hearth—for maybe eight shillings you'd have plates of mutton and chicken and bacon, pigeon-pies, bread and beer—"

"And the inns gathering places for duelists and courtesans . . . at least it kept them off the streets."

"Oh, come on! Wouldn't you give an arm and leg to set the clock back four hundred years if you could?"

"Set the clock back? No, thank you. Back to a day when goldsmiths were bankers and barbers were surgeons? To a day when streets were no wider than lanes, so that only two creaking carts could pass; and lanes were as narrow as public footpaths? When those overhanging upper stories that Americans find so quaint were needed for living space? When there were riots, fires, rabbit warrens of tenements, and the air was so fetid with pestilence that one had to draw curtains round one's bed to sleep through the night without getting the plague? When the constant refrain was 'Chattels and goods had he none'? Set the clock back? Don't be an idiot." Melrose drank his ale.

"Man, you're really on a downer."

"The entire sixteenth century was on a downer, my dear fellow. If you Americans had

had a taste of Elizabethan politics, you'd have applauded Nixon for being so forthcoming and upstanding."

"Nixon? That s.o.b.?"

Feeling he'd gained an advantage in a most unexpected quarter, Melrose smiled a wonderful smile and said, "Oh, I don't know. I've always thought of Richard Nixon as Mary, Queen of Scots."

"I can't believe it," said Harvey, looking sadly from his map of old Deptford up to the new, but seedy-looking, development. "Pepys Park. Can you feature it?"

"You didn't imagine, did you, that Deptford Strand would still be the site of duels and ruffs and painted ladies?"

"Well, yeah. But, I mean *really* . . ." He looked behind them, across the street. There was a pub called the Victoria. They had passed the John Evelyn a while back. "I mean, can you imagine turning the whole damned place into a bunch of *apartments*?"

"Yes." Melrose looked down at Harvey's map. "I see no Rose tavern there. Mistress Bull's."

Harvey scratched his head. "Well, no one knew where it was, exactly. Come on, let's keep walking."

"Let's go back to Brown's," said Melrose.

"Stop raining on my parade. Come on."

And they continued their walk toward the river.

"How about this place?" said Harvey, looking up at the tall facade of an unsavory-looking pub with a dull sliver of yellow on its sign announcing it as the Half-Moon.

"Good as any, I suppose. The original tavern belonging to your Mistress Bull is certainly gone by now."

"How do you know this wasn't it?" To one side was an alley no wider than a gutter. An unprofessionally lettered sign with an arrow pointed, apparently that way. "See, it says there's a garden out back."

"It's probably the way to Kew."

The building was decidedly ugly, its dark frontage running up into an overhanging upper story, giving it a listing and dropsical look. A large lattice of flaking green paint flanked one side of the door.

"The place must be old. That lattice used to be the sign of an ale house. They painted them red or green." Harvey was looking reverently at the ugly building, his cap crushed in his hands.

"Oh, for heaven's sake. You don't really think you're going to find the original, do you? Do you think it's still standing as a living memorial to your theory? Come on; I'm thirsty. Let's see if the happy host has some Old Peculier."

*   *   *

* * *

The inside was no more inviting than the outside. No light intruded by way of the leaded glass panes made still more opaque by a layer of grime. Down the length of the long bar, being slowly wiped down by the publican chewing on his cigar, ran a quite magnificent beveled mirror with a gold-leaf frame sporting cupids and Pans and other minor dieties probably doing things they'd no business doing in public. The few patrons—it was yet barely eleven in the morning—looked as if they'd been born in the place. They all seemed to have soaked up some of the darkness of the interior. From cigarettes, smoke rose in thin tendrils. The customers coughed. The room had a brackish, dead-fish smell. But there was the magnificence of the mirror and the old china beerpulls to salve the customers' souls. Not that these looked terribly soulful.

"Hiya," said Harvey, plunking some coins down. "Two of those." He pointed to one of the beerpulls. As the publican set up glasses, Harvey said, with his usual bonhomie, "Say, this wouldn't by chance be the old Rose tavern, would it?"

"The ol' wot, mate?" The owner squinted his eyes.

"Used to be a tavern in Deptford Strand they think was called the Rose. Run by one Eleanor Bull. Near as I can make out, it would have been around here. Christopher Marlowe was mur-

dered there." Harvey shoved Melrose's ale
down the bar and took a drink himself.

"Murder?" He went a little pale. "Wot you
talkin' about? 'Ere now, you be police, or wot?"

"Police? Who, *us?* No, no, no. You don't understand—"

Nor would he ever, thought Melrose with a
sigh, separating himself from the uncomfortable
wooden stool and taking his drink to a table. He
watched Harvey natter on. A dour-looking
woman who walked down the bar like someone
with springs on her feet joined in the discussion.
Harvey finally shrugged and came to join Melrose.

"They never heard of the Rose, or Eleanor, or
Marlowe. But they said in the back they did
have a couple of separate rooms for people who
wanted to have their own party. Come on, let's
check it out."

Harvey led the way down a narrow dark hall
at the end of which two doors debouched off to
the right and left onto identical rooms, furnished with round tables and chairs just as un-
inviting as the ones in the main bar. The only
other door led to the outside, with a sign on the
lintel, "Mind Your Head."

Minding their heads, they crouched and went
through into the garden, or what might at one
time in the dim, dead past have been a garden,
now gone to seed. An opening in the crumbling
stone wall led to the alley.

Melrose sat down on a listing bench as Harvey surveyed the scene, delighted. "It could have been just like this, Mel." And he started going through a director's motions, someone blocking out places on a stage, putting Kit there, Bob here. "I mean, can't you just see it?"

"No," said Melrose, charmingly. He yawned.

"Don't tell anyone," said Harvey, once they had gained possession of a table in the Half-Moon's dark public bar, "but I write a little poetry myself."

"Believe me," said Melrose, wondering if anyone had ever drowned in a glass of ale like the Duke of Clarence in a butt of Malmsey, "I won't tell anyone."

"Sonnets, mostly. Yes sir, I got them all in here." He patted the computer, drank his beer, and looked sidewise at Melrose. "Want to hear a line? 'If sands still bear the imprint of a sandal—'"

Melrose interrupted quickly. He would nip this recitation in the bud, even if it killed him. "Were I you, I'd stick to computer programming."

Sadly, Harvey shook his head. "You know what, Mel? You kind of take the bounce out of life."

"Not out of *your* life, surely. You'll still go bouncing along with no hindrance from me."

"What do you do for fun, anyway? You got a girl?"

"A 'girl'?"

"Yeah. You know." Harvey drew curves in the air.

"I know what they are. At the moment, unfortunately, no. You?"

He looked off across the small sea of dark, empty tables. "Once I did. Was going to get married. I didn't know her all that long. Love at first sight—for both of us." He sighed. " 'But that was in another country. And besides, the wench is dead.' "

Melrose was not at all surprised at Harvey's quoting Marlowe, but at the extremely un-Harvey-like bitterness in his tone. "I'm very sorry."

"Ah . . ." and the motion of his hand seemed to wave away wench, death, and that other country. "I don't brood. That's the worst thing you can do is brood. You get to the point you can't think of anything else, know what I mean? Listen—" Harvey smiled and slapped a pound note on the table. "Put up a quid—isn't that what they call them, 'quids'?"

"Quids, yes."

"Okay, now you put up a quid and we'll see who buys." Harvey raised his glass. "I'm betting you don't know who said this."

"Said what?" Melrose obediently unlayered a pound note from the wad in his money-clip.

" 'Who ever loved, that loved not at first sight?' "

Melrose frowned. "Good grief, every school-boy knows that line. It's Shakespeare."

Looking terribly smug, Harvey shook his head.

"Of course it is. Ye gods, haven't we all just seen *As You Like It* umpteen times? Touchstone says it."

"Uh-uh. Marlowe."

"Marlowe? Ho ho. You buy."

"Ho ho, *you* buy."

To Melrose's eternal annoyance, he leaned over and tapped away at the Ishi, waited a moment, brought up a file, and sat back, complaisance written all over his face.

Melrose leaned over and read:

> *It lies not in our power to love or hate,*
> *For will in us is overruled by fate . . .*
> *Where both deliberate, the love is slight,*
> *Who ever loved, that loved not at first sight.*

"From *Hero and Leander*," Harvey said, and lifted his glass. "You buy."

"Well, I'll be damned," said Melrose, without rancor. He was always willing to be educated, even by the Harvey Schoenbergs of this world. "You mean the bard stole it?" Melrose gathered up their glasses.

"Nah. He *quoted* it. Look at a text. It's in quotes." Harvey leaned across the table, said *sotto voce*, "Which is one more clue in my theory—"

"See you later," said Melrose quickly, making for the bar.

But of course, Harvey remembered his place quite perfectly. As Melrose set the pints down, Harvey repeated: ". . . one more clue." He started punching up the Ishi again, saying at the same time: "Far as I'm concerned, you put the sonnets together with the stuff from this play, and it adds up to one word. For example, look at this. Touchstone again: 'It strikes a man more dead than a great reckoning in a little room.' "

Melrose frowned. "Referring to what?"

"Marlowe's *murder*, of course. Don't you *remember*? 'Le reckenynge'—it's what the fight was over, the settling up of the bill in the tavern." He outflung his arm as if they were indeed sitting in that selfsame tavern. "Do you know that line about love at first sight is *the only time Shakespeare ever quoted another poet in his plays?*"

"So?"

"Ah, come *on*, Mel. Use your loaf, as they say over here. Marlowe's death is obviously really bugging the hell out of Shakespeare. Now put that together with everything else I've told you—"

Melrose was quite happy to have forgotten everything Harvey had told him in case it resulted in brain rot. He studied the massive and ornate gold-leaf mirror over the bar as tap, tap, tap went Harvey's nimble fingers on the Ishi.

"—together with the other sonnets, and *especially* this one." The screen scrolled up, Harvey banged a key in triumph, and read, " 'Farewell! Thou art too dear for my possessing—' "

Melrose, feeling displays of temper to be ungentlemanly, not to say emotionally depleting, was seldom given to them. But now he banged his walking stick down on the table, making both Harvey and the Ishi jump. "You go too far! *That* is probably one of the most beautiful sonnets ever written, and obviously written for some woman—the Dark Lady, probably . . ." His voice trailed off. Melrose really was not at all sure of his ground, but he refused to let this sonnet become grist for the Schoenberg Ishi. "The Dark Lady," he repeated. Why couldn't they talk about the French symbolists?

"Ah, don't be so romantic. It was Shakespeare's apologia, or whatever you call those things. Just wait till I tell all this to old Jonathan." Harvey's expression grew uncharacteristically dark. "He'll be in this afternoon. Concorde."

"Jonathan must have a bit of the ready." At Harvey's questioning look, Melrose added, "Money."

"Yeah. Well, the folks had it." Harvey brightened up and said, "But so do you, with a title to boot. Listen, come on and have dinner with us, okay?"

Melrose was curious enough about the

brother to agree. "You really dislike your brother, don't you?"

"No love lost on either side. But this Shakespeare-Marlowe business—I told you it could all be summed up in one word."

Blackly, Melrose regarded him; hating himself, he asked anyway. "What word?"

"Remorse. Billy-boy knows what he's done, and there's an end on it." Happily, Harvey drank his pint.

"I certainly *hope* there's an end on it." Melrose bethought himself. "Do you realize we've been sitting here talking about Marlowe's murder instead of these murders much closer to hand?" He looked at Harvey who was closing up the Ishi. "Tell me. You surely must have a theory on *that*."

Harvey shrugged. "Some nut. Who else could it be?"

"One of you."

Harvey stared at him.

And it was Melrose now who happily quaffed his ale.

24

.

"Honeycutt," said Wiggins, "is at the Salisbury pub."

"The Salisbury. He doesn't waste any time, does he? Well, come on then, we might as well join him."

The Ford idled away, seemingly forever, waiting for one of the green lights which never appeared to get one much farther round Piccadilly Circus and its eternal traffic snarl. In defiance of lights, laws, and even the knowledge that heavy metal can play hell with human flesh, pedestrians kept trying to make a break for it. One could hardly blame them, since all the cars were in competition with them, as if one and all were dicing to see who could get through the light first or last before it changed.

"Why don't they just take down the bloody lights and let's have a free-for-all," said Wiggins, nosing forward where three middle-aged ladies apparently didn't know or care how close they were to his bumper. The base of the statue of

Eros was crowded as usual with office workers and battalions of pigeons, all on their lunch-hour.

"Excepting Farraday himself, we're no clearer to a motive for any of these people than we were before. He might have murdered Amelia out of jealousy. Had plenty of reason, that's for sure. And might also have killed the stepdaughter, who was a real sexual tease, though that seems a thin motive—"

"What about the girl, Penny? She hated both of them." Wiggins had finally managed to leave the Circus for Shaftesbury Avenue, and was looking for a place to park.

"No," said Jury, in a tone that made Wiggins look rather sharply round. "That I can't believe. She's only fifteen."

Pulling the Ford up on the pavement in a sidestreet near the Salisbury, Wiggins clucked his tongue. "Only fifteen. Never thought I'd hear something like that from you, sir. Getting soft, are you?"

"Me and Attila the Hun," said Jury, climbing out of the car. "But that still doesn't explain the murder of Gwendolyn Bracegirdle."

"Why do they like turtlenecks so much?" asked Wiggins, once inside the Salisbury, which was jammed as usual at lunchtime. Although its clientele was diversified, it had a long-established reputation as catering for the gayer London crowd.

Wiggins was right; fifty percent of the crowd seemed to be wearing them. The young man at Valentine Honeycutt's table certainly was. Honeycutt had wasted no time. When Jury and Wiggins approached, he looked up and withdrew his hand from his friend's knee. The friend, tight-jeaned, turtlenecked, and sipping his beer, turned eagerly toward the new arrivals. Honeycutt wasn't quite so eager.

"Oh, no," he said with a sigh.

"The Bad News Bears," said Jury, not waiting to be asked to have a seat. He smiled at the young man, whose own teeth were whiter than snow and whose dark locks framed his smooth face, one would have said Byronically, except one knew Byron had other ideas. "Sergeant Wiggins, Mr. Honeycutt."

Catching on, the young man looked horribly sad, as if he'd hoped for better things at this unlooked-for expansion of their small party. Though he seemed to realize during his first lingering look at Jury's smile, that he wasn't Jury's type.

"Sorry to interrupt. We'd like a private word with Mr. Honeycutt."

Jury suffered a small, whispered conference between the two before the one in the turtleneck moved himself and his glass off. The jeans were decidedly constricting: Jury could almost hear splitting seams.

Honeycutt was dressed in his usual modish fashion: silky-leather jacket, silk scarf wound round his neck and waterfalling down his back, white cord pants. He only needed racing goggles. "What is it *now?*" he asked, as if Jury were nothing but a fun-spoiler.

"Mrs. Farraday. Amelia. I'm sorry to have to tell you, but she's met with an accident. Fatal."

"Oh, *God!*" he said, pushing himself against the back of the red banquette. Above him, on both sides of the slightly recessed seat, tulip-shaped wall sconces glowed. The Salisbury had one of the handsomest interiors of any London pub. "Where? *How?*"

Jury sidestepped that question with one of his own: "Were you at the hotel last night, Mr. Honeycutt?"

"Until around nine-thirty, ten-ish. Then I went to that little restaurant nearby, Tiddly-Dols." When he saw that Sergeant Wiggins was writing this down in his notebook, he frowned. "Why?"

"By yourself?"

"No, with a friend—look, why these questions?" His brief, nervous laugh was more of a high-pitched giggle. "You make it sound as if I need an alibi, or something. You surely don't suspect—"

Wiggins interrupted. "And what time did you leave Tiddly-Dols, sir?"

Honeycutt wrenched his gaze from Jury's and said, "Oh, I don't recall precisely. About eleven . . . But I still don't see—"

"Your friend's name, sir?" asked Wiggins, wetting the tip of his pencil with his tongue. Wiggins feared every ailment known to man except, apparently, lead poisoning.

Honeycutt opened his mouth and shut it again and returned his gaze to Jury.

Seeing he was getting into the noncooperative stage, Jury said to Wiggins, "How about getting us something at the hot-foods counter? Piece of shepherd's pie for me. And a pint of mild-and-bitter." Wiggins closed his notebook and got up. Jury smiled. "Haven't eaten yet today. Food's good here."

Honeycutt seemed to relax. After all, anyone about to eat shepherd's pie would hardly go for the jugular, would he?

"You still haven't told me how it happened, Superintendent."

"In Berkeley Square last night. Not far from that restaurant, as a matter of fact. About midnight, the police surgeon puts it at." Jury smiled again.

The jugular had definitely been gone for. Valentine Honeycutt went several degrees of pale. "You certainly don't think *I*—"

"Oh, I don't think anything at the moment.

But I imagine you can understand that we'd want to account for the movements of the only people in London—as far as we know—who knew her. They'd be the ones on Honeysuckle Tours. Thanks, Wiggins." The sergeant had set before him a steaming plate of minced beef topped with nicely browned mashed potatoes. He also put Jury's pint and a half-pint of Guinness on the table. "Aren't you eating, Wiggins?"

Wiggins shook his head. "Bit of a stomach upset." He had extracted a small foil-wrapped package from his coat pocket and proceeded to drop two white tablets into the Guinness.

Jury had thought his sergeant would never surprise him again, until he heard the fizz. "Alka-Seltzer in stout?"

"Oh, it's wonderful for digestion, sir. And Guinness is good for you." Wiggins reopened his notebook. The velvety foam of his glass erupted with little bubbles.

"Did you see any of the others on your tour last night? Or did your usual policy of laissez-faire still hold?" asked Jury.

"I saw some, yes. And if you're wondering precisely who was where, I suggest the first person you ask is Cholmondeley." His tone held a note of triumph as if he'd found the goose with the golden egg.

"Why's that?"

"Because he was meeting Amelia, that's why. Later that night." Honeycutt lit a cigarette.

"How do you know?"

"How? Because he told me."

Jury put down his fork. "I find that odd. He doesn't strike me as the sort who would go round confiding things like that to others."

" 'Confiding,' no. I don't expect he thought there was anything of 'confidence' in it. He told me very casually, after I asked him if he cared to have a go at one of the casinos with me." Honeycutt blushed and looked off, smoking delicately. He shrugged. "George simply said he was meeting Amelia." There was a pause before he added, while studying his perfectly polished nails, "I don't expect he knew Amelia was about to be murdered."

25

"Why is it that I always seem to be lunching with police?" asked George Cholmondeley, in a not-unfriendly tone, after acknowledging the introduction of Wiggins and waving toward the other chairs at his table.

"Sorry, Mr. Cholmondeley. The desk clerk at Brown's told us you were coming here. And it *is* rather important. I take it you haven't heard the news about Mrs. Farraday?"

A glass of wine poised at his lips, still he did not drink. Slowly he lowered it, pushing his plate back at the same time, as if the food no longer interested him. Jury noticed it interested Sergeant Wiggins, though, who was looking at the *tournedos Rossini* with considerable suspicion. Wiggins distrusted the more elaborate cuisines as he distrusted unfamiliar climates. It amazed Jury that someone with Wiggins's menu of maledictions still clung tenaciously to a steady diet of plaice, chips, and tinned peas.

"The news, I imagine, is extremely unpleasant. Or you wouldn't be here."

"Extremely."

"What happened?"

"She's been found murdered. I understand you told Honeycutt that you had an appointment with her?"

He allowed Cholmondeley to stall long enough to take out cigarettes, offer them around, light up. "Well, yes, as a matter of fact I did. Except a better way of putting it is that *she* asked to see *me*."

"Oh? And why was that?"

"Because she did not seem to understand that the flirtation was over."

"And was she making things difficult for you?"

"Difficult? You mean, embarrassing?" Cholmondeley laughed, and then apparently realized laughter was hardly appropriate in the circumstances. "Sorry. No, that wouldn't have happened. I think I see where you're heading, though."

Jury's face remained blank. "Do you? Then tell me and we'll both know."

Cholmondeley said nothing, only looked from Jury to Wiggins as if perhaps he might find a clue written on the sergeant's face as to where Cholmondeley most definitely didn't want to say he'd been the previous night. Wiggins was a brick wall when it came to giveaway expressions, however.

"You seem to be looking for motives. Mine would be a very slight one, believe me."

"Where were you meeting?"

"Berkeley Square. It's near the hotel, but not too near."

"Not very nice, meeting an unescorted lady in a park late at night."

"And who said it *was* late at night?" Cholmondeley calmly smoked and looked as if he'd scored a point.

"Merely an assumption. Her husband said she went out for a stroll after dinner. And that was sometime after nine-thirty. Nearly ten, I believe. Was she strolling with you?"

"No," said Cholmondeley curtly. "I told you, Amelia didn't turn up."

"Didn't turn up *when*, sir?" asked Wiggins, who had put down his notebook in order to unscrew a small vial of pills.

"Midnight. I know one or two clubs in the vicinity. I told her I'd take her."

Wiggins took the pill dry, under his tongue, and resumed his note-taking.

"That puts you in Berkeley Square around the time she was killed, Mr. Cholmondeley," said Jury.

"I never went *in* to Berkeley Square. I waited at the west entrance, where we were to meet. No, I have no witnesses, so I expect that makes me your prime target." Cholmondeley leaned across the table. "Only what possible motive could I have for murdering Amelia Farraday?"

"Perhaps what was mentioned before: she might have been uncomfortably persistent."

Cholmondeley's look was scornful, as if to say Jury should be able to come up with something better than that.

"Or maybe she knew something that might be even more embarrassing than this commonplace love affair. I'm still wondering why a man like you—a sophisticated and experienced traveler, and an Englishman—would want to join up with a group of Americans on a tour."

"I don't see why that bothers you."

"It does. According to your passport, you've been to the Continent five times already this year. To Amsterdam."

"What's odd in that? I've told you I'm a dealer in precious stones. I have to go on buying trips."

"I should think you'd be a bit sick of Amsterdam. This tour stops there for an entire week. And you could hardly be looking for someone to show you round London. Or Stratford, for that matter. You could go there anytime. I should think, if you wanted a holiday, you'd choose the Mediterranean, the Amalfi coast, the Côte d'Azur—something a bit different."

"Superintendent, you take *your* holiday on the Amalfi coast or wherever bloody well suits you. And leave me to take mine." Cholmondeley stuck his cigar in his mouth and reached toward his hip pocket. Apparently, he thought it was settling-up time.

"I would do, except I never seem to get a holiday. But when I do I don't make it a busman's holiday, like you."

Cholmondeley merely shook his head, extracted a very large note from a money clip and dropped it on the table.

Jury opened his own notebook. "The Amsterdam police have had a few talks with the gentleman you do business with, Paul VanDerness. Mr. VanDerness runs a legitimate shop. Most of the time. But on one or two occasions there's been some suspicion of black-marketing in diamonds."

"I don't believe it, but even if it were true, what's that to do with me?"

"I was just thinking, if one is on tour, as opposed to traveling alone, how the luggage is done. Honeycutt would have taken care of that particular drudgery for everyone. Just collected it all in a big heap and plunked it down for customs. A mountain of luggage. The Farradays probably had fifteen cases among them. Seeing as how it's only a bunch of Americans—and, for the most part, holiday-makers—the customs people might not even inspect it. Or just give it a cursory examination. If I wanted to take out diamonds illegally, I might join up with a tour."

Cholmondeley knocked ash from his cigar

with the little finger on which winked one of those diamonds in which he dealt, and said, "You'd better be careful, Superintendent. I have nothing more to say, except that my solicitors won't like this at all."

Jury said nothing. He knew that Cholmondeley would not be able to resist his own further defense.

Pocketing his cigar case, Cholmondeley went on. "So you've come up with the ridiculous notion that I told Amelia Farraday I was *smuggling diamonds* and that she threatened—oh, really, it's all too absurd."

Jury still said nothing.

"And what about the Bracegirdle woman? And Amelia's daughter? Was I going about indiscriminately 'slashing'—as the newspapers love to say—in order to keep them all quiet? Do you imagine they *all* knew about my alleged black-marketeering? It's unfortunate for me that Amelia isn't here to put an end to this nonsense."

After a while Jury broke his silence. "It's more unfortunate for Amelia."

"Do you really think that, sir?" asked Wiggins, when they were in the car and on their way back to Brown's Hotel.

"About the smuggling? I don't know. Never be able to prove it, I suppose. I took out a search warrant, but the men found nothing at all in his

digs. Not that I thought they would. Cholmondeley would have rid himself of whatever
contraband he brought over when they got back
to London the first time. Or maybe even in
Paris—I don't know. Shook him up a bit,
though."

"*Would* it provide enough of a motive?"

"Frankly, I doubt it. The lack of motive is the
worst thing about this case. Where are we without one? It might as *well* be the Yorkshire Slasher
we're dealing with. Indiscriminate killing. Only
we know it isn't indiscriminate." They drove in
silence for a moment along Piccadilly. "When
we get to the hotel, you see Cyclamen Dew and
I'll see the aunt. Haven't met her, have you?"
When Wiggins shook his head, Jury said, "I'll
bet it'd clear your sinuses up in a quick hurry.
What was that pill you took back there? It's a
new one."

Wiggins seemed pleased that Jury was keeping tabs on Wiggins's prescriptions. "A bit of
high blood pressure. Got a diastolic ten points
higher than it ought to be."

"Too bad. A pill a day, is it? My cousin's got
high blood pressure."

Making the turn up Albemarle Street, Wiggins was only too happy to fill Jury in. It was the
first really new illness that the sergeant had
managed to contract in several years. Until now,
he had had to settle for refining the old. "Doctor
says it's the job, you know. We're under too

much strain, we are, and it can't help but show. Now, you, well, I don't think you're quite so sensitive as me—" When Jury turned his head away quickly to study the glass facade of the Roller showrooms, Wiggins apparently felt he had leveled an unintended smart at his superior, and quickly added: "*Not* to suggest you're calloused, or anything like that. I only meant that I, well, I've always *felt* things so much more than most people. It's bound to have to come out some way, isn't it? We really sacrifice ourselves to this job, don't we?"

Wiggins should have a good time with Cyclamen Dew—a high old martyrdom for both of them.

". . . and it's such a terrible nuisance, having to take pills for something that's got no symptoms. I mean, when a person's in such otherwise good health."

Jury looked at him in open-mouthed amazement. But Wiggins's face was perfectly straight. Almost holy.

26

When Jury walked into the paneled lounge of Brown's Hotel, Lady Violet Dew was pouring something from a small flask into her cup of tea and reading a *Hustler*.

She looked up over the rim of the magazine and shoved up her glasses. "I only need them for reading," she said, slapping the magazine shut. She smiled—as well as she could, given the absence today of both uppers and downers—and looked at Jury appreciatively.

He had been similarly appraised the day before, when he had collided briefly with Lady Dew as the Honeysuckle Tours coach was readying itself for the jaunt between Stratford and London.

"Questions again. I heard all about it; the hotel's all agog; chambermaid's nearly scared out of her pants. Sex crimes are always the worst, aren't they? Probably because at bottom that's what everyone wants. Sit down, sit down." She patted the cretonne invitingly. "Have a cuppa? I'm buying."

Jury did a wonderful imitation of a man completely bushed who was all prepared to relax. He even loosened his tie. "I could use one, that's for certain."

"Bet you don't get much chance just to relax and have a bit of a natter, do you? Got to get home to the little wife and kiddies, I expect."

His smile was quite brilliant in the semidark of the bar. "No wife and no kiddies."

She gave him a playful slap on the arm. "*Go* on. A good-looker like you? Well, if you're single, all the policewomen must be stark ravers."

"Not quite all. I have my bit of fun, of course."

She moved a few inches closer. "Ever been to the States? Haven't seen anything till you've seen Hialeah racetrack. Play the ponies?"

"Why, Lady Dew—"

"Vi."

"Vi. You've already invited Mr. Plant."

"So what? The three of us could have a right old rave-up, don't you think we couldn't."

"I'm sure we could. In the meantime, how about answering a few questions?"

"Anything for you. Fire away!" She put her knobbled hand over Jury's.

"Where were you last night?"

"Where—?" For some reason, the implication of her being a suspect seemed to delight her; she laughed and slapped her thigh. "Wish I'd been out on the town, but there it is. I was all by my lonesome. In my room here."

"With Cyclamen?"

"No. Cyclamen went to the play with Farraday and the girl. All by myself, like I said. No witnesses. Just up there whacking away at my razor-strap."

"It's no joking matter. Aren't you at all afraid?"

"Would you be afraid if you'd just had three gins? And why would you think I'm afraid if you think I'm the guilty party? 'Where were you last night?'" She parodied Jury's low voice and intonation.

"Assuming you aren't, I should think you might feel queasy about three women on your tour having been murdered. Only the women, it seems."

"What about the boy, James Carlton? Do you think he's another victim? Only the body's not been found yet? Of course I'm afraid, you idiot. Why do think I'm down here drinking myself blind?" She motioned to the waiter for another cup.

"You say your niece went to the theatre?"

"Yes. Got back around eleven-thirty or midnight, so I can't give her an alibi. Maybe the others can—Farraday and the girl, Penny."

"Would she be capable of crimes like these?"

"Probably not. But I'd say the same about any of the others. There's Farraday and Schoenberg and Cholmondeley. I couldn't take odds on any of them. You don't really think a woman did them, do you? It's sex, take my word."

"There's no evidence of that. And if there were—it could still be a woman, couldn't it?"

"Odd sort of woman."

"Decidedly odd. Tell me about your niece, Lady Dew."

At that, she let go of the hand she had reclaimed, let it drop with a thud on the table. "Don't know what you mean."

"Sure you do." She wouldn't have made a good poker-player. Were it not for her stiffening defensiveness, Jury wouldn't have had any particular reason for believing that Cholmondeley was right about Cyclamen Dew.

When she said nothing, Jury prompted: "Gwendolyn Bracegirdle and Cyclamen were very friendly, according to some reports—"

"A damned lie!"

"What is?"

"That Cyclamen's—well, perverse."

"What about Miss Bracegirdle?"

"I don't speak ill of the dead," she said with questionable self-righteousness.

Jury smiled. Lady Dew would speak ill of anyone if it damned well suited her. All she needed was a little pushing. Although it was clear she wasn't all that fond of her niece, still she would probably think it a blot on her own sexuality if a female Dew were queer. Jury pulled the roll of magazines from his pocket.

"What's that?"

"Just some mags I was taking to a friend. The Dirty Squad cleaned up yesterday."

" 'Dirty Squad'? What's that?"

"Drugs and Pornography . . . Ah, ah!" Jury jerked them away as she outreached her arm. "Police evidence."

"Said you were taking them to a friend."

"Well, he's another policeman."

"Two of you going to sit and drool over them, that it? Disgusting, I call it."

"We all have to relax sometime." Flicking through the magazine, Jury let out a long, low whistle.

She was trying to twist around to have a look over his shoulder. He slapped the magazine shut. "Sorry."

"Damned bloody blackmail, that's what it is!" She snapped her mouth shut as the waiter set the fresh teapot down with Jury's cup. "All right, what if Cyclamen does like her bit of fun that way? Who'm I to look down my nose, though it beats me how she could—and with that Bracegirdle person. So dull. I wonder which of them was the, you know, and which . . . ? Well, that sort of thing goes on all the time and no one thinks anything of it. Look at the Honey-cutt person. Idiot. To each his own."

Jury handed over the magazines. "Your niece and Miss Bracegirdle used to 'go off' for periods of time. Did they go to the plays together in Stratford at all?"

"Not to my knowledge. That night I thought Cyclamen went to bed with a sick headache, but of course I don't know. Here now, what are you suggesting?"

"Nothing, really." Perhaps he oughtn't to have handed over the magazines before he got her answers; she was trying to look at the çenterfold, forgetting Jury. "In other words, she might have been out on the night Gwendolyn Bracegirdle was murdered, and also out last night. Lady Dew?"

"Eh? Oh. Yes, I suppose so. None of us have alibis." She seemed to think this rather rich. "Never been married. Um. How old are you, lad?"

"Forty-three. Not so young, after all."

"Ha! Just you wait'll you get to be sixty-two like me. *Then* you'll think it's young."

Even if he hadn't seen all of their passports, Jury would have known she was in her eighties.

But at the moment, he felt very old.

Penny Farraday pushed her shirttail into her jeans and smoothed down her hair.

"This is Detective Sergeant Wiggins, Penny. C.I.D."

She held out her hand. "I'm pleased."

"How do you do, miss?" said Wiggins.

"I'm sorry, Penny. But we need to ask you

some questions. You went to the theatre last night with Mr. Farraday and Cyclamen Dew?"

"Yeah, that's right," she said in a lackluster voice. Picking up a magazine, she absently thumbed through its pages.

"What time did you get back here?"

"Ten-thirty, maybe eleven. Amelia"—her hand froze in the act of turning a page and then went on—"was supposed to go too, only she changed her mind when we got to the theatre and said she was just going to walk around. I think He was pretty mad. Can't say I blame Him." Nervously, she tossed the magazine on the table. "It was *The Changeling*. It was good. You know what a changeling is?" Despite Jury's nod, she went on to explain: "A changeling's when you put the wrong little kid secretly in place of another one." She frowned and continued her explanation by means of extrapolation: "It's like stealing kids and pretending they're your own. It's not *quite* the same thing as adopting—"

Jury could see where this sort of thing was leading. He had to interrupt. "Mr. Farraday did go out last night, then?"

She was still frowning, probably over awful thoughts of changelings. "Yeah. But if you're looking to make Him out to be guilty, well, you're just crazy. *He'd* never do nothing like that. Never."

"You seem quite certain."

"I am. That's not to say I hold with everything He does—" she added quickly.

"What about Miss Dew?"

Penny shrugged. "I reckon she went to bed."

"Did you see her aunt? Or any of the others? Cholmondeley? Schoenberg?"

Penny looked up, studying the ceiling, hands clasped behind her head. "Nope. That dumb Harvey was over across the river . . . said he was going to see Southwark Cathedral."

"But that would have been earlier."

"I guess." Penny put her head in her hand. Whether she was upset about Amelia or merely bored with the questioning was difficult to say. But when she finally looked up at Jury, the cause of the anxious look in her eye was plain: "What about Jimmy? There ain't no one looking for Jimmy, not with all this other going on." And in a small voice she said, "Jimmy's dead, ain't he?"

"No," said Jury. "If he were, we'd know by now. And don't think we've stopped looking. The Warwickshire police are combing the county."

Jury only hoped, looking down at the girl, his instincts were right.

27

The books were stacked on the floor in a heap.

James Carlton had taken the top board—about five feet long—and shoved it up onto the top of the bureau. After he got up there himself, he turned it and slid it through the opening made when the bar had finally given way. Since the opening wasn't as wide as the board, he had to angle it, which made maneuvering the far end across to the branch very hard work. He was sweating and at one point was certain he'd lost his grip and that the board would fall and that would be the end of things. But it didn't; he managed to balance the opposite end on the straight branch to form a walkway. The end he had hold of he positioned on the several inches of thick stone that protruded out from the wall of the house. It seemed steady enough. He inched through the opening and leaned on it as well as he could, and it still seemed quite stout and steady. Of course, it wasn't much of a test; it was hardly the same as putting his entire weight on it. He looked up at the sky; he was glad it was nearly pitch-black. There was only that little bit of chill moonlight which iced the upper branches of the tree opposite.

The gray cat, sitting on the bureau beside him, apparently thought all of this work was being done for its personal amusement. It slipped through the opening and promenaded back and forth across the board, from sill to branch, ending up on the heavy branch and starting to claw away at the tree trunk.

It was 4 A.M. James Carlton had timed his escape for long enough before it got light so that he could get away in the dark, but close enough to first light so that he would not have to walk too far in the dark. Also, it was an hour when people—he didn't know how many—would be bound to be asleep.

James Carlton crouched down and thrust his legs through the opening first; then, using the bars for leverage, he wiggled and pushed until the rest of him was through, half on and half off the sill and board. He went very slowly so as not to jostle the board from its position. Finally, he was all the way out, his legs dangling over the edge of the sill. He did not look down as he carefully hoisted his weight up until he could stand on the ledge, holding fast to the bars behind him.

The board had moved only a fraction of an inch. After all (he told himself), it was only a few feet over there to that branch. Two long strides and he'd be in the tree with the cat. But still he gripped the bars, looking up at the dark sky and the cold stars, feeling the terrible void of the night all around him.

On the branch, the gray cat sat, ghostly in the moonlight. It seemed to think this nocturnal start on a tree house decidedly more of a lark than lying curled up on James Carlton's bed. *Get on with it*, it urged.

But James Carlton's fingers were frozen around the bars, as the stars, when he looked up, seemed frozen in place. He wondered if God had shut down the universe. Was his watch still going? Was his heart? Or had everything that ticked stopped?

Maybe he should pray, he thought, looking at the board spanning a space wide as the universe he had just looked up at. He didn't have to empty his mind—it seemed part of the void. But he didn't know what prayer to say. And then his mind started to fill up with images. His father, the war correspondent–flying ace–baseball player. Undoubtedly, his father had been a crack parachutist too . . . His father wouldn't be proud of him . . . nor would the Man in the Iron Mask, who probably wouldn't even need a board. He'd jump.

One finger unfroze and stuck itself in his back. The tip of a sword. In his mind he heard a band of voices singing *"Yo ho ho and a bottle of rum . . ."* And then one voice—cruel, salty, rum-soaked,—yelling, *"Well, me hearty! You'll be din-ner for the fishes tonight!"*

The finger punched him harder in the back. There was nothing he could do. He had no choice. Either be run through or take his chances with the sharks. . . . Beneath him the dark water churned and foamed and the fins circled and he could see his own blood rise to the surface. . . .

He was in the tree almost before he knew he'd let go of the bars.

Now there was getting down the tree, no trick at all for James Carlton, who'd climbed most of the trees in West Virginia and Maryland.

But for the gray cat, it was something else again. Walking the plank was one thing; going down a tree was another.

If James Carlton hadn't yanked and tugged, he figured the cat would have sat up there all night, howling at the moon.

They both landed in a heap on the soft earth at the base of the trunk.

The house was as dark as the night beyond the trees. James Carlton, the cat padding at his heels, backed off first to get a good look. The house rose tall, cold, and heavy as the prison it had felt like inside. Nothing moved; no lights shone. And then he saw, around the back of the house, a pale wash of light. He crept quietly. Standing back, he could see into the lighted window. There was a man's figure moving about in there.

James Carlton didn't hang around to introduce himself. He picked up the cat and ran.

28

Melrose Plant settled himself in the lounge in roughly the same spot that Lady Violet Dew had recently vacated, and in roughly the same shape as Jury, who sat next to him.

"Where's Schoenberg?" asked Jury, without preamble.

"Dear God, will you just let me take the weight off my abused, if well-shod feet before you start in?"

"No," said Jury, motioning to the waiter, who must have been preparing himself for an endless stream of tea-drinkers on this particular sofa.

"He's still out running round Pepys Park, I expect. That's a nice-looking display of sandwiches. Agatha would die—" He outreached his hand for a triangle of watercress.

"What's Pepys Park?"

Melrose sighed. "It is the development put up some few years ago by our city fathers on the site, presumably, of Marlowe's old Deptford Strand. Harvey wept, of course. But that's the way it goes. Progress, progress." Melrose took another triangle, this one of fishy-stuff, from the tiered plate.

"What time did you leave?"

"I'd say around 1586—why?"

When Jury told him what had happened to Amelia Farraday, Melrose stopped eating, was silent for some moments, and then answered Jury's questions more seriously: "We left the hotel about nine. We had breakfast together."

Jury thought for a moment. "Whoever murdered Amelia Farraday was taking a chance, coming back to the hotel in the early hours. Wiggins says that none of the staff saw any of our little tour group come in after midnight. Except Cholmondeley. But we knew that, anyway."

"I don't know. The place has entrances on two streets. I've walked in the other one and I don't think anyone's noticed me. Or at least until I was well inside."

"But you couldn't *depend* on that. It's taking a chance."

Plant looked at him. "It's taking a chance to murder someone, old chap."

Jury smiled slightly. "True." He fell silent and then said, tiredly, "We haven't talked with Harvey yet. When's he coming back?"

"Fairly soon, I expect. He's supposed to meet his brother Jonathan for dinner. The brother's getting in sometime this afternoon. Concorde, he said."

"Expensive," said Jury. "He must not be hurting for money."

"Well, as I take it, he got what there was of the family graft. I'm invited to dine, incidentally, but I—"

"Terrific," said Jury, rising. "You can ask Harvey the right questions. And to make sure you're up to the mark, I'll just have Wiggins stop along for coffee. Schoenberg shouldn't be too laid up with jet-lag."

Melrose's smile was sour. "Thanks awfully. You don't suppose they're *alike*, do you? Can you imagine talking with two of them?" Melrose replaced his teacup. "You know there's something I've been wanting to mention—" He shrugged. "I don't know. It can wait."

"I'm going back to the Yard. I want to talk to Lasko, among other things."

Jury left.

Melrose sat there wondering if perhaps he should have, indeed, mentioned it after all. But it seemed a bit frivolous to be talking about the relationship between Thomas Nashe and Christopher Marlowe at this point; Jury would think Plant had been driven slowly mad by Harvey Schoenberg. *Perhaps*, thought Melrose, *I have*.

"Nothing," said Lasko, talking to Jury from Stratford-upon-Avon. "We've been over this whole area ten times, checked all the buses, trains—everything we could think of. No sign of the kid."

Even over the telephone, the hangdog look of Lasko was visible. Jury told him what had happened to Amelia Farraday. There was something slightly less-than-sincere in Lasko's reactions. Jury still thought Sammy was glad it hadn't happened in Stratford. He could hardly blame him. "Keep checking on Jimmy Farraday." It was all Jury could think to say before he replaced the receiver. Racer's cat (they had all come to think of the cat that patrolled the halls that way) had narrowed a passage through Jury's office door and around Jury's spartan furnishings and between his legs and, finally, streaked up to his desk as if it were following a beam of light.

Perhaps they took one another's measure until midnight. The documents in the case he had already sifted over and sifted over and come up with nothing new—there *was* nothing new. . . .

Unless one could count the dispatch sent that afternoon from Chief Superintendent Racer with its usual perfunctory address:

"Jury. Although I haven't heard from you in the last several hours, it has come to my attention that another murder has taken place and that you have not seen fit to report to me immediately. Why I find this unusual is, perhaps, due to my own thwarted idea of—"

And there followed—fortunately, Jury thought, not in Racer's actual person—the usual castigations, imprecations, and variations upon the theme of Jury's fallibility, ending with a command to report in at dawn. The firing squad will have loaded up by then, he supposed, tossing the paper aside.

The cat, finished washing, cast its eyes on the memo and yawned.

Jury read the poem and reread it. That he could not make out its connection to these murders made him feel an utter fool. Nothing beyond the fact that they had all been women, and the pertinent stanza certainly dealt with that sad knowledge. But he could add to that something else: the stanza dealt with the passing of Beauty. Fair queens. Helen of Troy. The dying flower. The death of beautiful women. Jury looked up from the poem to the blank wall. Gwendolyn Bracegirdle had not been beautiful at all—well padded and permed, middle-aged at thirty-five. Had it not been for Gwendolyn, Jury would have been certain someone had it in for the Farraday family.

From the papers on his desk he pulled the passport of James Farraday and looked at the tiny picture. From that he looked to the blow-up of that part of the passport which contained James Carlton's face. He looked again at the passport—Jimmy with James Farraday and Amelia—and thought how intelligent the kid looked. He stared at it for a while longer, then picked up the telephone again.

"Airports?" said a sleepy Lasko. "Well, hell, no. Why'd he ever be taken out of the country? . . . Look, Richard. I hate to say it but you and I know that kid must be lying dead out in some field we just haven't stumbled into yet—"

Jury interrupted. "No, he isn't."

Lasko sighed. "Just how in the *hell* are you so sure of that?"

Jury wasn't. "The victims have all been women, Sammy."

"But they'd need documents, Richard, to get out of the country."

"It's not impossible to come by passports, Sam. Anyway, if you want me, I'll be at my place." He gave Lasko his number in Islington, hung up, and swiveled round to stare at the black pane of his window.

It had to be the Farradays. The Farraday women. There was only one left. Penny.

"Mr. Jury—"

It was Mrs. Wasserman from the basement flat in Jury's building, standing in his doorway, clutching her dark robe together at the neck, and holding out that day's—or yesterday's— news.

Her hand, Jury saw, was shaking. "Come on in, Mrs. Wasserman." He did not ask her why she was up at this (for her) ungodly hour. He already knew. Probably she had been watching from behind her dark-curtained window through the long day and longer night for the policeman who lived upstairs to come home. She often did.

She stepped in, still bunching the robe together, and quickly shut the door, keeping the other hand behind her on the knob as she leaned against the door.

Jury hid a smile. It was so like a bit from an old Bette Davis film, an actress's pose. But Mrs. Wasserman wasn't acting, Jury knew, as he looked down at one of the racier London tabloids where even the usual front-page undressed girl had had to give place to news of "The Slasher." If Mrs. Wasserman, somewhat *deshabille* herself, could walk up two flights of stairs at one in the morning, then she was nervous indeed.

British newspapers had always done a creditable job of cooperating with police by keeping the gorier details of killings out of the news. It was necessary for the simple reason that there were too many potential Slashers out there, waiting for a modus operandi to be disclosed so that they could grab a piece of the publicity. But this particular paper was skirting much too closely around the edges of that pool of blood in which lay the body of Amelia Farraday. Oh, it left something to the imagination, granted. But constant repetitions of "mutilation" would set even a less-imaginative person than Mrs. Wasserman on the edge of her seat.

" 'The Slasher'—what a terrible name. Somewhere, Mr. Jury, somewhere he's out there. Walking about, someone who looks like anyone. . . ."

Jury was afraid it would simply add to her storehouse of fears to learn that The Slasher might well be a woman. Mrs. Wasserman knew the dangers of men, or so she thought. So entrenched in paranoia was she, that Jury had helped her again and again with new bolts for her door, new grilles for her windows, new locks, keys, chains. And new lies. He did not know how many stories he had made up about the infallibility of the Metropolitan Police Force when it came to protecting women walking down the street.

He knew she heard, barricaded there in her basement flat, an army of marching feet in the occasional step of the passerby on the pavement, and in that army was always her pursuer, the Feet that stopped, the Form that lurked, the Shadow on the pavement. Jury could see in her mind all of the carefully chosen paraphernalia symbolizing safety—the bolts, the locks, the chains—all melt in some Daliesque landscape and run like dark blood down her door.

His expression had given something away.

"I'm right, Mr. Jury. So dangerous it is, even to walk out—"

Firmly, he took her arm and sat her down in his leather chair, the one good piece of furniture in the room. "No. You're wrong." He tossed the paper in which one could almost smell blood mix with newsprint over to his desk, out of her reach. "I'll tell you why you're wrong, but only if you promise not to buy another paper tomorrow. Promise."

She clasped her hands in her lap and nodded. "I promise." Then she smiled her sad, schoolmistressy smile and shook her finger at him. "But we both know, don't we, Mr. Jury, how you can't tell me anything. Even though it's you in charge. The paper says so." This last she said almost proudly, as if Jury were the young relative who'd finally proved he wasn't a good-for-nothing.

"Forget about that. I can tell you this much: this person they're calling The Slasher and trying to make out is prowling all over London—absolutely untrue. He's not going about indiscriminately killing wom—people. He knows exactly who and what he's after, and it's got nothing to do with strangers, or all of London, or anyone else."

She believed him. She always did. Only this time, he was happy to report to himself, it was all true. It almost made *him* feel the truth was coming closer. Jury smiled his first genuinely felt smile of the day.

At that her face wore the look of the drowner finally breaking the surface of the water.

Air, it seemed to say. *Thank God*.

29

Jury winked at Fiona Clingmore, who stopped in the act of showing herself her recently varnished nails, to show Jury something more important. Fiona repositioned breasts and legs and rested her carefully made-up face on her interlaced fingers. "You're late." She slid her glance toward Chief Superintendent Racer's door.

"As far as he's concerned, I always am."

Jury shoved the door open (just in time to see Racer apparently adjusting his hairpiece, which didn't help the entrance), strode across to the chair near Racer's desk, settled himself more or less on his spine, smiled, and said, "Hi."

Racer, even the hairpiece forgotten at this, stared at Jury as if he'd gone mad. "I beg your pardon, *Superintendent?*"

"Why?" Jury looked at Racer out of innocent eyes—clear, soft, dove-gray. He knew it wasn't worth it to try to drive Racer a little farther round the twist, but the temptation was hardly one he had to go looking for.

"*Why?*" Blood the shade of his carnation boutonniere suffused Racer's face. "We do not address our superiors with a 'Hi.'"

"Oh. Sorry. Sir," Jury added as a well-timed afterthought.

Racer leaned back, regarding Jury with the suspicion a police officer generally reserves for somewhat more criminal game, and said, "You'll go too far one of these days, Jury."

Since Jury had gone too far too long ago even to remember, the comment seemed somewhat redundant. "You wanted to see me?"

"*Of course* I wanted to see you. Yesterday. This Farraday woman. Another American cut down in the streets and the American consulate wants to know what the hell's going on. Understandable. So what's going on, Jury?"

"If you're asking me, have I solved this series of crimes? No."

"I am asking, Superintendent, for a report," said Racer through clenched teeth.

Jury gave it to him, the state of Amelia Farraday's corpse, in bloody detail. ". . . somewhere between eleven and shortly after midnight. Twelve-thirty, perhaps."

"Motive?" snapped Racer.

"If I knew that, I'd be dancing in the streets."

"Wiggins?" Racer had of late taken to this elliptical manner of speech, no doubt to frustrate those under him even more.

Jury frowned. "What about him?"

"What's he doing, man? Besides infecting

everything in sight." Racer looked down at the papers on his desk—seldom were there any— and gave Jury a kind of side-swipe grin, like a misthrown punch. "All of these snatches of poetry. The plague. Sergeant Wiggins is well suited to the case." Racer sat back, prepared to instruct. "Been reading up on it. 'Lord, have mercy upon us' was something they wrote on doors." Racer made a movement with his index finger, as if the air were his door and he wished Jury behind it. "Did you know there were signs, they thought, that signified the coming of the plague? Same sorts of signs I see when Wiggins walks down the hall—toads with long tails, great numbers of small frogs, that sort of thing." Racer coughed.

"Hope you're not getting—"

Jury stopped short of condolences. Some buried thought had almost surfaced during Chief Superintendent Racer's lecture. Was it possible Racer had actually said something helpful?

"A bit snide, I thought," said Wiggins, as they drove down Piccadilly. They had been talking about Jonathan Schoenberg. Wiggins fell silent, squeezing the car between two double-decker buses that seemed to be racing each other past Green Park.

"Well? What do you think of him?" Jury prompted.

Wiggins was taking out his small tablecloth of a handkerchief. His nose was twitching, rabbit-wise, though not (Jury feared) on a scent. "Who, sir? Harvey or the brother?"

"We *know* Harvey like a second skin. Jonathan, of course."

"He looks like—" Wiggins was overcome by such a violent attack of sneezing that Jury had to grab the wheel to keep the car on course.

"Sorry, sir. But have you ever noticed how Green Park sets off an allergy this time of year?" Wiggins blew his nose and turned up Albemarle Street.

"Can't say I have. Go on about the brother."

"I was just saying they look alike, but they certainly don't act anything alike. Harvey spends a lot of time waving his fork, the brother eats with his. You know what I mean."

Jury smiled. "Yes. What did Mr. Plant think?"

"Same as I did. He thought this Jonathan seemed a bit of a cold fish. The brother's contemptuous of Harvey. I don't think they go down a treat with each other. Professional jealousy, I'd say."

"Hard to think of anyone's being jealous of Harvey. Professionally or otherwise."

"I'd say the jealousy part's the other way round. This Jonathan's a professor of English literature. Teaches at a college in Virginia called St. Mary's. And spends most of his time over here in the British Museum reading old manuscripts." Wiggins pulled up to the curb in front of Brown's, stuck his head out of the window, and shouted a silver Mercedes out of the way.

They sat in the car for a few minutes. "How did Schoenberg react to these murders?"

Wiggins shrugged. "Like I said, pretty cold-blooded. Ivory tower sort. He said he thought it was shocking, of course. Frankly, I think it'd take a lot to make him worry about his brother. Or anyone else, for that matter."

As they slid out of their respective doors, Jury said, "I can hardly wait to meet him."

"I think it's revenge," said Jury, in Melrose Plant's sitting room at the hotel.

Plant frowned. "Why not gain?"

"The psychology's wrong. These killings are all too—I don't know—ritualistic."

"Revenge against which of them, though, on the tour? It would be a pretty clear-cut case against the Farradays—or James Farraday—except for the murder of Gwendolyn Bracegirdle. That's the facer, wouldn't you say?" asked Plant.

Jury nodded. "I would indeed. Maybe she got in the way."

Plant grimaced. "Sloppy."

Jury shrugged. "Nothing's perfect."

"Revenge. It makes me think of what Harvey said, a rather stupid comment—well, perhaps not so stupid—about *Hamlet*. 'Revenge tragedy.

One's just like another. You go round killing off
all the wrong people until you finally manage
to kill the right one.' Hard to think of our murderer trying to work up the nerve to kill his own
particular Claudius." Plant smiled grimly. "If
all of this were directed at the Farradays, I'd be
very nervous for Penny."

Jury felt cold. "Mind?" He helped himself to
a tot of brandy from Melrose's decanter. "Want
some?"

"Yes, I could use one." Melrose looked at his
watch. "Well, it is at least afternoon. Agatha
thinks I'm racing toward alcoholism. The only
positive side of all this is that it's made her
afraid to come to London. Cheers." Melrose
raised his glass.

"Where's Schoenberg? Did you see him this
morning?"

"In Deptford, naturally . . . oh, you mean the
brother?" At Jury's nod, Melrose said, "The
British Museum, of course. They left together."

"What'd you think of brother Jonathan?"

"Icy. He certainly doesn't take his brother seriously."

"Have you seen Penny?" When Plant shook
his head, Jury said, "I don't want Penny leaving
the damned hotel."

He said it with such vehemence that Melrose
almost jumped. "If you don't want them moving about, you'll have to place them in what-do-
you-call-it? Protective custody."

"Penny I should lock in a closet." Jury drained his glass and stood up.

"Where're you going?"

"To see Jonathan Schoenberg."

As he walked toward the door, Plant's voice stopped him. "Look, there's a small thing—"

Jury turned. "What small thing?"

"Well, it probably doesn't mean anything, but it's that damnable poem. It's by Thomas Nashe."

Jury came back into the room. "Believe me, I know by now who wrote it."

"Well, that's just it, old chap," said Melrose, also draining his glass. "What I can't figure out is, why didn't Harvey Schoenberg?"

The silence in the room was palpable. Then Jury said. "What do you mean?"

"For example: I showed it to the brother, Jonathan. He recognized it almost immediately. Especially because of that line, 'Brightness falls from the air.' "

"Schoenberg's head of an English Department—it's his . . ." Jury stopped.

"That's right. You were about to say 'speciality.' But look at it this way—which you obviously are, judging from your face—Jonathan Schoenberg knows his Shakespeare, I'm sure. And Marlowe. But I'll give you odds he can't hold a candle to Harvey when it comes to mere facts. Thomas Nashe *was one of Christopher Mar-*

lowe's best friends. You haven't had the benefit of
hearing Harvey doing his Elizabethan name-
dropping bit. I went to the Stratford library.
Harvey had been telling me all sorts of really es-
oteric stuff that happened in Marlowe's life.
Marlowe was well known for brawls and duels.
Harvey told me all about them. There was one
street brawl in Hog Lane that turned into a
duel. Harvey knew all of the people involved.
But if he knew all the others, he'd certainly have
known Nashe was there. Nashe is a thread in-
terwoven in Marlowe's whole life. He even
wrote an elegy, *On Marlowe's Untimely Death*—"

Plant stopped, lit a small cigar and looked up
at Jury. "The point is old chap . . . well, why did
he lie?"

"Miss Farraday?" By now the pretty receptionist was getting so used to police on the
premises, she scarcely stiffened with interest. "I
believe she went out, Superintendent. But I'll
certainly try her room."

There was no answer.

Across the Thames in the Half-Moon tavern,
the publican was wishing it were Time. Hardly
any custom this afternoon, except for the boys
in the public bar, where he still kept the drink a
penny cheaper. They were a rowdy lot.

Bored with the afternoon's takings and leav-
ings, he had a drink himself and then walked

down the hall to the gents. As he did so, he happened to look into the empty room to the left of the toilets and wondered why the missus had left on the dim overhead light. He reached in to switch it off. His eyes bulged.

All twelve stone of him fainted dead away.

30

Before Wiggins had brought the police car to a stop, Jury had the door open and one foot on the curb, already lined with cars from R Division. Several uniformed policemen had cordoned off the spot, keeping back the knot of people who always seemed to gather for state occasions, accidents, and murders.

"Back here, Superintendent," said the sergeant who had, he said, been the one to put in the call.

The wall of divisional police were creating more of a traffic hazard inside than were the curious, outside. Jury was introduced to Detective Inspector Hatch of R Division, who led him down the dimly lit corridor to a room on the left.

Jury had been so certain of what he would find that he had spent the drive across the Southwark Bridge steeling himself against visions of her mutilated body. He could not, at first, take in the fact that the victim was not Penny Farraday.

The body in the chair, arms dangling and head thrown back from the brutal blows to the face, was the body of Harvey Schoenberg. The pulpy mess that had once been Schoenberg's eyes made Jury think that in some Oedipal fury, Harvey had turned a sword upon himself. And what appeared to Jury as almost the saddest note in this Grand Guignol of blood-soaked clothes was that some of the blood had run down the blind-eyed screen of Harvey's little computer.

The police doctor was shutting up his bag. "Hello, Superintendent. As you can see, it wasn't too difficult to determine the cause of death. The throat partially slit—funny, almost like an afterthought—the other thing went straight through to the brain. Interesting how the killer came by this weapon." The doctor held out a handkerchief-covered hand on which rested a dagger. "Rather medieval, wouldn't you say?"

"Elizabethan," answered Jury.

The doctor looked both surprised and mildly amused. "I must say you fellows are certainly up on weaponry." He lapped the handkerchief over the dagger. "He's been dead under two hours. No sign of rigor at all." The doctor was putting on his raincoat. "Hope you'll forgive me; I've done all I can here, and I just missed the second act of a very good Webster. *The White Devil.*"

The yellow, metal-shaded light overhead cast

gloomy shadows across the table. "Those revenge tragedies are all alike."

Surprised, the doctor said, "I wouldn't say that."

"It's something he said."

The doctor turned to look again at the body of Harvey Schoenberg. "You knew him, then? Well, I suppose that makes your job much easier."

"Much." Jury wasn't smiling.

No one in the pub, according to DI Hatch, had seen the murdered man come in.

"He must have come in by way of the alley and the garden. The owner remembers seeing him in here yesterday with another man. Says he was asking questions about some old tavern, the Rose. Said it used to be around here. He"— Hatch gestured toward the chair that had lately held the body of Harvey Schoenberg—"must have come in after the eleven o'clock opening, given what the doc said. We need to find that other man, the one he was with—"

"I know the other man."

Hatch looked at Jury as if the superintendent had second sight. "So. Last of all," said DI Hatch, handing over the scrap of paper, "this."

Even as his hand reached out for it, Jury knew what it was:

> *I am sick, I must die.*
> *Lord, have mercy upon us.*

"Reads like a damned suicide note. Obviously not suicide though. What's it mean? Any idea?"

"It's the end of a poem."

At least Jury hoped it was the end.

"Because I wanted to see Southwark Cathedral," said Penny Farraday, who appeared to be having no trouble facing down an extremely irritated CID superintendent.

After Jury had told her about Harvey Schoenberg, she had gone into her room and slammed the door, stayed for a few minutes, and then returned, her face slightly mottled, all trace of tears scrubbed away.

Still, she said nothing about Harvey Schoenberg. The argument was over her own wanderings over London. "I mean—shiiiiit!—we ain't *prisoners* . . . we ain't been *arrested*—"

"Southwark Cathedral," said Jury. "When did you suddenly develop this religious streak?"

Penny slumped on the sofa beside Melrose Plant, whose refusal to glitter when they had finally met had not helped her attitude. "Since old Harvey—well, look, I'm sorry he's—anyway, since he told me the story about it." She grabbed up a pillow and punched it a few times and then stuffed it behind her back, as if her fury were aimed at the furniture itself.

"A story. If you want to hear a story, *I'll* tell you a story. I'll toss you in the nick and tell you a very *long* story about why I don't want you walking round London *on your own.* There's plenty of blokes up alleyways with plenty of fascinating stories for little girls—"

"I *ain't* no little girl—"

Jury merely overrode her objection by raising his voice: "And most especially, I don't want you going anywhere with *anyone* connected with this tour! Is that clear?"

She lowered her eyes and lapsed into grim silence.

Jury repeated his question: *"Is that clear, Penny?"*

Sharply her head came up as she yelled at him, *"You* ain't my daddy!"

The face seemed blistered with anger. But the tone was not truly heartfelt.

"What story?" asked Melrose, after Jury had left the room to go to Scotland Yard.

Peevishly, she said, "It don't matter. God, that's ~~four~~ of us been killed now. And then there's Jimmy! Whatever *did* happen to Jimmy?" Again she picked up the down pillow and held it against herself like soft armor. "I try and tell myself, it ain't nothing but he just run off. But you *know* it's got to be more'n that."

To keep her from dwelling on this morbid possibility, and also because he was curious, Melrose insisted she tell him Harvey's story.

"Oh, it was just about this girl, Mary Overs. She had this daddy named John Overs who ran the ferry over the River Thames and got rich because he was the only one with a ferryboat. But he was real cheap and *mean*." Biting round her thumbnail, Penny scrunched down farther into her corner of the sofa, as if sinking into the very depths of meanness herself. She kicked off her loafers. "This John, he was so cheap he kept Mary hid away because he didn't want no boys seeing her. She was so beautiful, see, any boy saw her'd fall in love with her like that." Penny snapped her fingers. "If they fell in love, that'd mean they'd want to get married and old John, he'd have to pay a dowry."

Melrose felt the way she squinted at him was to see if he fully understood how heartless this exacting of dowries was.

She continued. "Her daddy, John, decided to pretend he was dead for a day jut so he could save the cost of feeding her servants. That's how cheap he was. But what happened was, they were so happy he was dead, they broke into the food and liquor and had a swell time, right there around his corpse. Or what they thought was his corpse. Then John rose up in his shroud to stop them, and, of course, they thought it must be the devil doing it and they run John straight through with a sword." Penny made a sudden thrusting motion. "Then Mary was free and when her lover was galloping to see her, his horse turned over and he broke his neck. Poor

Mary was so heartbroken she turned a nun and started this priory, St. Mary Overies—"

"Which later became Southwark Cathedral."

Penny looked up at him, surprised. "How'd you know that?"

Melrose shrugged. "I'm a schoolteacher."

Her surprise turned to something resembling disgust, as she said, *"Schoolteacher!* How can you be a earl and be a schoolteacher?"

"I'm not an earl," said Melrose, absently. He was turning over the details of the account Jury had given him of the murder of Harvey Schoenberg, and thinking that it was more than strange; it didn't add up.

"Not an *earl?*" Penny was indignant. "But *he* told me—" She pointed toward the door through which Jury (that liar) had recently walked.

"Sorry. I gave up my title under an act of Parliament passed in 1963. The Impoverished Earls Act, we could call it."

His smile was directed at a (for a change) nearly speechless Penny. She could but get out the single word: "Why?"

"Because."

" 'Because'—that ain't no answer. You don't just give up being a—"

But Melrose was thinking of his earlier conversation with Harvey. " 'When surgeons were barbers,' " he said, reflectively. "Southwark . . ."

Penny had apparently grown as sick of South-

wark Cathedral as had Melrose of his earldom.
"Then that means your wife can't be—what? An
earless?"

"Countess."

Disgust was written all over her face now.
"You mean to tell me—Godamighty!—that you
gave up your wife being a *countess*, too?" Penny
toed her loafer and punched at the silken pillow.
"How selfish can you get?"

Melrose picked up his walking stick, prepara-
tory to leaving, and sighted down it. "Well, since
I have no wife, it makes no odds, does it?"

At this, she bit her lip, and finally said, "Well,
I can damn well tell you this: if somebody I was
in love with was to die, I sure wouldn't be a *nun*
over him!"

Thus they sat there for another moment or
two in semi-companionable silence, reflecting
on the loss of Harvey Schoenberg, the peerage,
and the possible repercussions in the state of
West Virginia.

31

It was not so much the brown eyes, untidy mustache, and weariness of posture that distinguished Jonathan Schoenberg from his brother—for the resemblance between them was clear—as it was the coldness of manner. Harvey's effervescence was completely lacking in the elder brother, like champagne gone flat.

They found him in the British Museum, where Jonathan Schoenberg's shoulders seemed weighed down with the dust of the antiquities around him.

"Dead." It might have been their surroundings—sarcophagi, Egyptian busts—that gave the word such a hollow sound when Schoenberg said it. The man seemed at a loss for some appropriate response. The stoop of the shoulders deepened, but neither the eyes nor the voice betrayed any particular emotion. "I can't believe it. I just saw him this morning—" He shook his head.

"You left Brown's Hotel together?"

Jonathan Schoenberg nodded. "He was going

to Southwark, no, Deptford. He had this obses-
sion about Christopher Marlowe."

"Yes. We know. Look, perhaps we could go
down to the Museum café and talk." The coldness of his surroundings was beginning to bear
down on Jury. He could almost see his breath.

Schoenberg sat with his cup of coffee and
loosened the knitted tie he was wearing. It
looked expensive, as did the suit, though
Jonathan Schoenberg did nothing to show them
off. It was as if the weight of the man's mind,
which Jury judged to be formidable, bore down
on the body, like a weight on shoulders, tie, cuffs
of trousers. Beside him, poor Harvey would
have looked almost spiffy.

"You're a scholar, Mr. Schoenberg. Was there
anything at all in your brother's research that
someone might have been interested in?"

"Interested—?" Schoenberg laughed briefly.
"My God, Superintendent, it was a perfectly absurd theory. What are you suggesting? That
someone killed him for it?" Schoenberg studied
his hands, laced across his knees. His tone was
so dismissive of the notion, that the man did not
appear to feel it needed the reinforcement of a
look at either Jury or Wiggins.

"Your brother had no enemies, insofar as you
know?"

"Certainly not enough for *that*. But it's hard to

imagine Harvey's really incurring anyone's rancor." He smiled slightly.

It was a smile, nonetheless. "Any hard feelings between the two of you?"

Schoenberg seemed amazed. He almost laughed. "Why would I harbor hard feelings about *Harvey*?"

Apparently, Schoenberg's coldness was grating on Wiggins, too, who pushed the cough drop on which he was sucking to the rear of his mouth and said, "We don't know, do we? That's why we're asking."

Jonathan Schoenberg seemed disinclined even to acknowledge Wiggins's existence, probably in the same way he would have ignored the presence of a younger, less perceptive colleague. Thus, he still addressed Jury. "Very well. Yes, Harvey appeared to be jealous. I was the one with the brains; I was the one favored by our parents; I was the one who got most of whatever was handed around. Harvey expended a great deal of energy in trying to prove himself, and I'm quite sure this whole *idée fixe* about Marlowe and Shakespeare was part of that." This was announced without much interest in Harvey's theory or in Harvey himself. Schoenberg spoke tonelessly as he examined the dun-colored walls, the lackluster fittings.

Perhaps that's what academic life did to one, thought Jury.

"Did you see your brother often, Mr. Schoenberg?"

Jonathan shook his head. "Seldom."

"But you don't live that far apart."

"True."

"Still, you met in London."

Schoenberg's head came up sharply. "So? I come here at least once a year, usually in the summer." He tossed his passport on the table, then went on in his passionless voice. "Probably he wanted to show me all of this evidence he'd collected." His smile was cold. "Or show me up. But given what's been going on—Harvey's theories about Marlowe and Shakespeare rather had to take a back seat, didn't they? I'm talking about the murders of the people on this tour he was on." Schoenberg looked at Jury as if he might have better ways of spending his time.

Since Jury had been about to ask to see the passport, he imagined that Schoenberg felt he was one up. Jury flicked through the pages. The visas had been stamped at nearly the same time every year for the last five years. Despite what Jury had said to Lasko, the passport looked authentic enough. Jury returned it to him.

"I imagine Harvey told you about the methods of this murderer." Jury took his copy of the poem from his pocket, the one stanza circled, and handed it to Schoenberg. "Sergeant Wiggins says you recognized the poem."

" 'Brightness falls from the air' . . . of course. It's one of Nashe's. That line alone is famous."

"He wrote the poem during the plague years."

Jonathan once more gave his small, superior smile. "Yes, I know."

Jury waited for Schoenberg to go on, but he didn't. Jury reclaimed and repocketed the poem.

Schoenberg, thought Jury, was about the coldest fish he'd ever landed. Or, more to the point, not landed. He couldn't make the man out at all.

32

"Poor Harvey," said Melrose Plant. "The silly ass was beginning to grow on me." With a feeling akin to nostalgia, he had been telling Jury and Wiggins about their travels round Deptford. He put aside the stapled pages he had been reading. "And doesn't this rather shoot holes in the Beautiful Women theory?"

"Thanks for reminding me," said Jury, rubbing his eyes and leaning back in his chair in Plant's sitting room at Brown's. The three of them—Jury, Plant, and Wiggins—had a printout from Harvey Schoenberg's computer, pried from the unwilling Ishi by a very frustrated computer expert at New Scotland Yard. Schoenberg had recorded over sixty pages on his trip and had, presumably, left even more at home.

Jury tossed his own set of stapled pages aside and said, "I've gone through this three times now and I can't find a bloody clue."

"I didn't know this," said Wiggins.

"Didn't know what?" asked Jury.

"How disgusting these public executions were. He's talking here about how people reveled in the twitchings of the body. They'd actually scream to the hangman to cut out the heart." Wiggins looked a bit ill. "And the hangman would leave them semiconscious and then cut them up and take out their—I mean, *sir*, how could anyone still be alive if—"

"Try not to think about it, Wiggins," said Jury, gloomily.

Melrose had finished reading the last sheet of his copy and said, "Anyway, the world has got more civilized, Sergeant Wiggins. Now all we do is hover over traffic accidents and ambulances."

"I certainly wouldn't call what happened to Schoenberg or any of the others in this case 'civilized,'" said Wiggins, testily. Illness, sickness, disease—Wiggins could not give it such short shrift. "And back then, in Marlowe's time, the plague. God, can you imagine anything more horrible . . . ?" Wiggins shuddered.

Jury raised his head slowly from a hand that wasn't doing much toward curing his headache and said, "'The plague full swift goes by.' Read that stanza, will you?" he asked Melrose.

Plant put on his spectacles and read:

> "*Rich men, trust not in wealth,*
> *Gold cannot buy you health;*
> *Physic himself must fade;*
> *All things to end are made;*

The plague full swift goes by;
    I am sick, I must die."

Jury looked at Melrose and said, "In all of that talk with Harvey—you said there was a woman—"

"Ah, yes." 'But that was in another country. / And besides the wench is dead.' "

Following his own train of thought, to Wiggins Jury said, "You might just have something there, Wiggins."

Wiggins looked around the room as if he might discover where the Something was. "Sir?"

"The public executions. The disemboweling. And how what happened to these victims was hardly any more civilized."

Jury got up. That elusive thought which had nearly come to him in Racer's office surfaced now. "We've been concentrating on that other stanza—the one the murderer left, and ignoring what the whole poem's about." Jury made a movement toward the door.

"Where are you going, sir?"

"To see James Farraday. I must be blind. I forgot the one person who's really important."

Melrose removed his glasses. "I must be dim. What 'one person'?"

"Their mother," said Jury.

"Nell?" said James Farraday. "What about her?" He was drinking what was obviously not his first whiskey in the elegant dining room of Brown's Hotel. "I don't understand."

"Just tell me what you know about her, Mr. Farraday," said Jury.

"But—she's dead." Farraday stuffed a black cigar in his mouth, which he then forgot to light.

"I know that. Penny said her mother died of what Penny called 'a wasting disease.' She was vague about what the disease actually was. I don't think she knew. So what was it?"

There was a long silence, and then Farraday said, "VD." He paused. "Syphilis." He seemed to be looking everywhere—out the window, at his glass of whiskey—"It's not exactly something you want to tell kids, is it?"

"No."

"Nell was just an ignorant little farm girl, was all. It went on too long, you know? By the time the doctor told me, it was too goddamn late." The cigar he'd been holding he finally lit. "She had to go to a hospital. More like a sanatorium, it was. Nothing they could do except make her comfortable as they could. Comfortable. Hell. You ever seen anyone with syphilis?"

"What did you tell Penny and Jimmy?"

"Told them she died, that's all."

That's all. Jury found it strange that the mother's death could merit that sort of dismissal. "And how did she get it, Mr. Farraday?"

"You're thinking *me*, right? Well, it wasn't me, Superintendent. She slept around, I guess. Listen. When I found Nell Altman she was near to walking the streets looking for work, and her with them two kids. And a lot of thanks I ever got from *them*, I can tell you—"

It did not seem so much self-pity as delay, Jury thought. "When you found out she was syphilitic, there must have been questions—"

" 'Must have been—' That's real funny. You're goddamn *right* I asked questions. Which she wouldn't answer. You never knew Nell. Lord, but that was one stubborn woman."

"If she told you nothing, why did you assume she 'slept around'?" Jury felt an irrational impulse to defend this woman's character. "It could as easily have been her husband who—"

"Husband? Don't think there ever *was* one."

"Okay. Then whatever label you want to give the gentleman—"

"I'll give the goddamn *gentleman* a label. Son-abitch is what I'll give him!" Farraday leaned across the table, allowing Jury the benefit of his whiskey-laden breath. "That bastard had VD and *never told her.*"

"Maybe he didn't know, either."

"And maybe he *did*, mister! Maybe he just didn't want to *trouble* her with that bit of information. Maybe he just didn't want the *bother.*"

"So what did you assume happened to the father?"

Farraday shrugged. "Lord only knows. Guess he just took off from her or something. She never

said. I never asked. And where she got that stinking disease, I don't know." Farraday ran his hand
over his face. "Poor bitch slept around because
she was so stupid about men she couldn't tell—"

"She slept around, but not with you, is that it?"

Farraday was silent for a moment. Then he
said, "I'd of married her. I mean, before I
knew . . ." His voice trailed off.

White of you, thought Jury, irritated by his unprofessional anger.

But it evaporated when Farraday said, sadly,
"She wouldn't have me. Don't ask me about the
father, or husband, or whatever. She was from
some godforsaken place in West Virginia—you
know the kind—blink and you miss it—some-
place called Sand Flats, something like that. All
I know about the girl's family is this dad of hers
who come around to get money off her—" Farraday raised his glass, as if to toast Nell Altman's father, but actually to call the waiter, who
appeared like swansdown at his side. "Ain't you
got any good old Kentucky *bourbon* in this
place?"

"Not Kentucky. Tennessee sour mash. Would
that be acceptable, sir?"

Farraday nodded and the waiter withdrew.
"Softhearted, Nell was. I shouldn't have said
that before, about her being stupid. Nell wasn't
stupid. Far from it. Gullible, that's the word.
Anyone could of got anything out of her. Like
that old grief of a dad of hers—"

"What was his name?"

Farraday looked up from the plate he was pushing food around on, confused. "His name?"

"I mean, was it Altman? Was Nell Altman using her maiden name?"

He thought for a moment and then said, "Yeah. I guess she was. You got to understand, Nell never talked much about herself—"

"Go on."

"Penny's like her. Looks like her, acts like her. Oh, Penny tries to sound hard, but inside she's like mashed potatoes. And that Jimmy—wherever did he get his brains? It wasn't the schools. I tried sending him to private school—well, it was Amelia thought of that." He wiped his napkin over his face, in what Jury thought was a surreptitious gesture to stop tears. Then he laughed artificially. "But Jimmy didn't take to private schools any more than public. We used to have this kind of joke, Jimmy and me: 'There wasn't a school made yet could hold Jimmy Farraday.' But Amelia, of course, she wanted all of them in private schools. That Honey Belle—it surely didn't matter there; she could of turned any school into a row of cellblocks. Penny, now that's different. The girl likes to talk like she just come up out of a mine. . . . But I think that's a kind of loyalty. . . . You know what I mean?" Farraday had received and downed most of his whiskey at this point.

"I know what you mean. Why wouldn't Nell Altman marry you?"

Farraday stared into his glass for a moment before answering. "She didn't love me, is why. Nell wouldn't've married anybody for money." Here he looked quickly away as if to keep Jury from seeing an expression that would betray a thought, *not like some*. Then he looked back. "There's no good me pretending Amelia and me were a couple of lovebirds. We had problems. There was a divorce coming up, sure as God made little green apples."

"I didn't know that."

"Neither did she," said Farraday, his voice low. "I guess it's not too smart, me telling you that after what's happened."

Jury smiled slightly. "Mr. Farraday, the police would have one hell of a time if every man who wanted to divorce his wife decided to murder her instead. Anyway, that would hardly account for the others."

"I'm not thinking too straight."

"Straight enough. Go on."

"Look. Don't think I wouldn't give *everything* I got to undo what's happened to Amelia and Honey Belle and the others. I guess I seem pretty coldblooded, but believe me, I'd give it all, and I got a lot. But to tell the truth—" He stopped and looked at Jury almost with entreaty. "—it sounds pretty hard . . ."

"The truth usually is."

"It's really Jimmy I feel grief over. And Penny. Nothing's happened to her *yet*—"

The word hung in the air, cold and sharp as an icicle.

"We'll find Jimmy," said Jury, with a conviction he didn't feel. But the man had been through a lot. "As for Penny, she's got orders not to leave the hotel, unless one of us is with her."

Farraday managed a laugh. "Penny. Never knew her to pay attention to *anyone's* orders."

"She will to mine," said Jury, smiling.

In a very low voice, James Farraday said, "You fellows . . . I don't think you're any nearer to knowing what's going on than you ever were." It was said not as an accusation, but rather as a gloomy foreboding.

Jury did not comment. Instead he asked another question. "Would you have said Nell was beautiful?"

Farraday seemed to be considering this carefully. "To me she was." He paused. "It was the way she was. I'd of thought she'd be beautiful to anyone, to tell the truth."

Jury got up. "As to what you said before—yes, I think we're closer to finding a solution. At least I've found a motive. Nell—that's a nickname. Wasn't her name really Helen?"

"Helen. That's right." But his look reflected only an increase of puzzlement. "Helen."

33

He had walked through woods (probably in circles) and down a long avenue (seeing only a few cars at this early hour), determined to get to the other side of that river he had seen from the tower room. There was a distant sound of traffic.

James Carlton was keeping out of sight as much as possible, carrying the cat weak from a lack of Jell-O (probably). Off to his right was bright green grass. At first he thought it was a golf course.

He walked over the brow of a hill and saw row after row after row of gravestones. James Carlton didn't know there were that many dead in the world. Row after row. And down there, way off, was a little band of people.

Then he heard it. Someone was playing Taps. He thought it only happened in movies.

With the cat draped over one arm, James Carlton stood as straight as he could and saluted. It was the slowest, most mournful sound he'd ever heard in his life. And as if someone had run a bayonet straight through his heart, he knew for a certainty that his dad was dead.

His dad wasn't a baseball player, or anything like that: his dad died a hero. And then he thought: maybe that funny vision of Sissy running past dead people and blood and gunfire was some old memory swimming up from a dark place in his mind . . .

The gray cat gave a small growl of discomfort.

James Carlton turned and left the place and kept on toward the river.

He'd just have to accept it: his dad was dead, so there was only J.C. Farraday to take his place. Well, that wasn't *too* bad. But he'd jump into a flaming pit before he'd ever take that Amelia Blue.

Anyway, his real mom was in Hollywood, maybe.

Maybe she even still remembered he was missing.

By the time he reached the bridge over the river, it was full light. James Carlton turned up the first street he came to. He was still carrying the cat, afraid to put it down because of the cars.

He asked a man with gray hair, dressed in tight jeans and a ring in one ear, where the police station was. The man seemed to sway slightly, as if to some music in his head, and said he didn't know if there was one. The street was a commercial one—full of fancy-looking stores and delicatessens—all still shut up and some with grilles pulled across their fronts.

The next person James Carlton asked was an old man bent over a trashbin, who didn't seem to understand the question and asked him for money.

Finally, he got a response from a solid, matronly looking woman in white, who he thought must be a nurse and who said, yes, she knew, but why did *he* want to know, and was he in trouble? She towered over him, a white mountain, full of questions and nursey-niceness, which reminded him of his old housekeeper. He told her no, nothing was wrong. He told her that his father was the chief of police and, having confounded her with this bit of news, he embroidered upon it by saying that the cat had been hit by a car. The gray cat, as if conspiring with his benefactor in order to find sanctuary, gave a pathetic *mee-ow*.

No stranger to accident, illness, and tragedy, the woman hurriedly pointed up the street, told him the various turnings, and wished him luck. She gave the cat a little pat before they parted and James Carlton walked on.

When James Carlton Farraday finally walked into the Georgetown branch of the Washington, D.C. Metropolitan Police Department, the handsome black officer on desk duty looked up and gave him a lavish smile.

James Carlton had always known that the police loved lost kids and animals, so he had no hesitation at all about launching into his story:

"My name's James Carlton Farraday and my daddy—I mean my *step*daddy—is James C. Farraday. He's in Stratford-upon-Avon. That's in England. I been kidnapped for five days."

As he continued his saga, the smile on the handsome policeman's face turned first to disbelief, then to astonishment. He did, however, make careful notes. Finally, in a tone that grated on James Carlton's nerves, he told him what a brave boy he'd been and what an exciting, romantic adventure he'd had.

"There ain't nothing *romantic* about it. You don't believe me, there's proof all written down on the back of a picture over in that house—" Here he pointed in a direction toward the Potomac River. "I been kidnapped five days and so's this here cat—" And he held it up to demonstrate what a kidnapped cat looked like.

Exasperated beyond belief and as close to tears as he'd ever been, James Carlton said in a voice louder than he needed to: "You got any Jell-O in this here jail?"

34

Jonathan Schoenberg opened his door at Brown's Hotel to Jury, Wiggins, and Melrose Plant, but failed to register any particular interest in another visit from the police, nor curiosity about their having brought along someone unofficial.

"A few more questions, Mr. Schoenberg," said Jury, who remained standing while the other three sat down, Schoenberg in his same place on the sofa, Plant and Wiggins in wing chairs. Brown's did not stint on the furnishing of its sitting rooms.

"All of this bitterness between you and your brother—"

"The bitterness was on Harvey's side, Superintendent."

"Yes. But I was just wondering—could we add to that, women?"

Jonathan seemed a bit surprised. " 'Women'?"

"One particular woman—"

Schoenberg laughed. "Look, oughtn't you to

be asking questions more germane to Harvey's murder?"

"I think this is. You've never been married."

"What on earth—?" He shrugged. "No. Why commit oneself to one woman for life? You don't have to marry a woman to have one." He slumped back against the couch, pulled the knot of his tie down even farther, as if it reminded him too much of the marital yoke. "I've never met the woman who was worth it."

Jury looked past him, toward the darkening window, the shadows muting the outlines of chairs and tables. "And did Harvey feel the same way?"

"Harvey? How should *I* know?"

"There's the larger question. The murders of the other three."

"Then you've got a homicidal maniac on your hands, Superintendent." Schoenberg lit a fresh cigarette from the butt of the old one.

"I don't think so." He nodded toward Melrose. "You've met Mr. Plant, here. He's got an interesting theory—"

"I'd rather see a little *action* out of Scotland Yard than sitting around listening to all this theorizing."

"The death of Christopher Marlowe—" began Melrose. He didn't get very far before Schoenberg laughed again.

"Harvey's got you doing it too?"

"In a way. Bear with me."

Grandly, Schoenberg waved his hand. "Fire away. I thought I'd heard every detail of the death of Marlowe."

Plant smiled slightly. "Given motive and opportunity, you knew enough to make your brother's murder look very much like Marlowe's."

Schoenberg's smile was thin as a blade. "But there wasn't motive, and unless you think someone else killed the others—I was in the United States. A dozen people can testify to that."

"I'm sure they can," said Jury.

Schoenberg looked at him.

"You know," said Melrose Plant, "that whole Nashe business is interesting."

"I don't find it so, but I daresay you'll tell me what you mean."

"Yes. But first, there is a rather intriguing notion about his death. One your brother didn't mention—oddly enough." Melrose held up the pages of the computer printout. "It's all in here."

"Well, well. And what have you got there? The name of the killer?"

Wiggins took a paper from his pocket. "You might say so, sir." Wiggins's voice rasped, not from a sore throat for a change.

Plant continued: "*Originally*, it was reported that Marlowe died in 1593 of what they called the 'grand disease'—the bubonic plague. Interesting that during the next fifteen years, it was only Marlowe's *enemies* who apparently circulated that story of his being killed in the tavern in Deptford. His friends didn't take this account seriously at all. The name of one Christopher Morley was written into the coroner's report. Now, Morley was quite a common name. And in those times the variants of the spelling of a name made it frightfully confusing when one was trying to identify documents. Shakespeare spelled his name several different ways—"

Impatiently, Schoenberg shifted on the sofa and said, "For God's sake, I know there were different spellings; I've been teaching the stuff for years."

"Marlowe occasionally signed himself 'Morley'—but only up to a certain time, and not after. Then he used 'Marley' or some other variation on the spelling of 'Marlowe.' There was, however, *another* 'Christopher Morley,' and one who just happened to be a confidential agent running between England and the Netherlands. Now, as to the others: Robert Poley, one of the three involved, was supposed to have been in The Hague on the day of Marlowe's death. That means he must have come to Deptford secretly. There were also *two* Nicholas Skeres—at least two—and written into the coroner's report was the name, *'Francis* Frazir.' Not 'Ingram'—"

Schoenberg at last registered anger. "What in the *hell* has this to do with Harvey?"

"If I could just finish?" Melrose lit one of his thin cigars. "It's perfectly possible that the person his enemies claimed was Christopher Marlowe was not the person killed in that tavern in Deptford Strand. And that Marlowe did, indeed, die of something else."

"There were sixteen jurors who identified the body," said Jonathan.

Melrose smiled. "You learned a lot from your brother. But that would have been a difficult identification, in view of the victim's having been stabbed in the face."

"Then why didn't Marlowe come forth and deny it?" In spite of himself, Schoenberg seemed fascinated.

"Simple. Political intrigue. He was told to lie low—"

"And then return from the dead?"

"Christopher Marlowe could have committed suicide." Melrose smoked his cigar. "He had plenty of reason. Newgate prison. Tom Watson's death. Betrayal by his best friend, Walsingham. Christopher Marlowe must have been a young man in terrible despair. Suicide would not have been at all unlikely."

Schoenberg threw up his hands. "Wonderful. Now you've solved the death of Christopher Marlowe. Would you kindly tell me what his relationship is to Harvey? Are you telling me my brother killed himself?"

Melrose raised a quizzical eyebrow. "Didn't you get the point, then, old chap? It was the misidentification of the body."

*   *   *

There was a long silence until Jury broke it by saying, "Absence of motive is always the most difficult thing in any case. Until we knew what the motive was, there just wasn't any connection between all of these murders. Nell Altman was the connection. But I don't think, really, it was Farraday who betrayed her. It was your brother. Correct?"

For several moments, Schoenberg seemed to be studying the pattern in the carpet. When he finally spoke, his voice had a totally different tone and timbre. "*Farraday* tossed her out, didn't he? Let her die in that goddamned hospital—"

" 'But that was in another country, / And besides, the wench is dead,' " quoted Melrose Plant, sadly.

"It was a class act, Harvey," said Jury. "You ought to be on the stage. The only problem was the eyes, wasn't it? Nearly the same height, same coloring, add a bit of a stoop to the posture, easy enough to put on a mustache, and to use the same razor for both the surgery and taking off Jonathan's. Pretty macabre, but it wouldn't have taken more than a minute. And it was easy enough to change gray eyes to brown with lenses. But you could hardly change the color of your brother's eyes. All of this material collected on the death of Marlowe—it was done so you could stimulate his murder and drag that red herring across our path. You could even allow us to suspect Jonathan, who'd heard 'every detail,' as you said. You must have studied your brother awfully intensely to get his movements, his voice down so well. Did you make tapes?"

Harvey Schoenberg said nothing. He pulled at the knitted tie again, as if he were strangling.

"You don't like ties, do you?" said Melrose Plant. "You were always fooling with those bow-ties you wore, too. I must say, it showed a hell of a lot of nerve, Harvey, to invite *me* along to meet your brother. But then you had to make sure you were seen together by someone who knew you. To get back to Thomas Nashe, Harvey. You tripped up there. Better to have admitted you knew that poem, because Thomas Nashe was one of Marlowe's friends, one of his greatest admirers. He said he 'knew no diviner muse' than Christopher Marlowe. He *collaborated* on *Dido* with Marlowe. Obviously, anyone who knew the minutiae of Marlowe's life would have known that, and would have known that famous poem."

Wiggins took from his pocket a photostated document, cleared his throat, and read, "James Carlton Altman, born June 1974 in St. Mary's, Virginia. Father's name given as Jonathan Altman." Wiggins regarded Harvey Schoenberg as coldly as he might have a new virus under a microscope. "Probably, she didn't want to give a different last name for the child. Embarrassing for her, and for him, of course."

"Where's Jimmy Farraday, Harvey?" asked Jury.

Harvey's head came up sharply. "*Altman*, you mean. Jimmy Altman—" He stopped, his gaze once again on the pattern in the carpet.

The silence went on long enough for Melrose and Wiggins to look up at Jury, who finally said, "I know Jimmy's in the Washington, D.C. area. Concorde only takes four hours. You could have got him over there and got back in one day, no one the wiser. Jimmy was always 'going off'; and no one kept tabs on the comings and goings of the rest of you. The Stratford police have already circulated your picture and Jimmy's. That flight leaves London at eleven forty-five A.M. and gets into D.C. at eleven A.M. Two hours later another Concorde flight leaves Dulles in Washington. At least two crew members on this side recall a sleeping boy with his father. We've already gotten in touch with the Washington police and the police in Virginia."

Harvey's head seemed to have been dropping steadily, like a man nodding off. Now it was in his hands. Jury's voice, low enough at the beginning, was now even lower, as he said, "Look, Harvey. We could sew the whole story together, I guess, but there'd be seams. You did all this because of Nell Altman, because she'd been deceived, betrayed—and my guess is—seduced by

Jonathan ... and I guess you thought, Farraday, too." Jury was silent for a moment. "You loved her."

Harvey's voice, changed by tears, larynx seeming to strangle a shout, came from somewhere between sofa and rug. *"You're goddamn right I loved her!"* His head came up. "Jonathan took her away from me like everything else. I knew Helen—Penny wasn't much more than a baby then—and I wanted to marry her, before Jonathan came along, the dirty bastard. He was always like that with women. Poor Helen..." Harvey's head dropped in his hands.

Jury's silence was so monumental that Wiggins finally broke in and said, "This vendetta against Farraday, though—"

"He let her die, goddamnit! And I can tell you this. I thought maybe he should have a taste of it, himself. Those two were *sluts*—listen, I finally put a private detective on Helen, that was after she disappeared with the baby. It was years. Years." There was a long pause. "I waited too long. She was dead."

Melrose Plant said, quickly, "She'd have died anyway, Harvey. Somewhere along the line she picked up syphilis."

"Farraday."

Jury shook his head. "No. Not Farraday. And what did Gwendolyn Bracegirdle have to do with James Farraday?"

"Nothing. Except she had a big mouth. And

she saw the resemblance. Faces. She kept on about how much Jimmy looked like me. Looked like Jonathan, I should say, only Gwen didn't know that. I could hardly carry out this plan with *her* around. I shut her up."

"And what did you have planned for Penny Farraday?" asked Wiggins.

Harvey looked at him as if he were a stranger. " 'Planned'? You think I would hurt Penny? That's Helen's *daughter!*" He slumped back on the sofa, his arm across his forehead. "Nothing. Jimmy—well, that's something else. Jimmy and I got on like a house-afire. Jimmy, I could have convinced . . ."

Silence again. Finally, it was Wiggins who asked, "Of what?"

But the fleeting smile on Harvey's face suggested that his thoughts were not in that room. "Of course, I had to give him something to make him sleep. From Stratford to Heathrow—I got ahold of a rental car—and then on the plane. But, boy, could that kid *sleep.* Once he woke up on the plane and was watching the movie." Harvey chuckled, as if he'd forgotten everything except Jimmy Farraday. "That kid had more imagination. He was like Helen—" Then he pulled himself out of the dream and said, "I had to give him another injection. . . ." He ran his hand over the back of his neck, frowning as if in an effort of remembrance, as if he, indeed, had been asleep for a long time. "He's at my house.

It's in Virginia. Other side of the Potomac. Place I bought when I got this little idea. An old stone place in the woods and a room up high with bars. Kind of like a tiny castle. A kid would get a kick out of that, wouldn't he? Guy that lives there I found to take care of it because he's sort of witless. Anyway, you pay people, pay them enough, they'll do anything. So when I got Jimmy there I just told him the kid was kind of sick and to not let him out and leave plenty of food for him. That I'd be back in a few days . . ." His eyes traveled over the faces of the other three, but did not seem to focus. "Farraday . . ." Now he sounded as if he'd lost interest in his own conversation.

Melrose Plant said, "I think you found your own Claudius when you finally killed your brother."

Harvey Schoenberg did not respond.

Jury looked at him for a few moments. Then he said, "Take care of things, Wiggins," and left the room.

35

James Carlton Farraday stood in Dulles Airport with the tall, black policeman for whom he had formed a definite attachment ever since the officer—Sergeant Poole—had actually gone out and found some Jell-O.

"I told him, miss," said Sergeant Poole to the flight attendant. "But he doesn't believe me." Sergeant Poole looked down at the cat-carrier, one designed to meet all of the specifications of air travel. The gray cat was grooming itself, as certain of its privilege as was James Carlton.

The young lady in the uniform of British Airways knelt down (James Carlton wished grown-up women would simply talk to him from up where they stood) and smiled (he also wished they wouldn't look sticky that way) and said, "It's too bad, dear, it really is; but the United Kingdom just won't let animals into the country."

James Carlton sighed. "Now that's about the silliest thing I ever *did* hear. There's more cats in England than anywhere I ever seen—saw, I mean. You going to tell me they was all *born* over there?"

The flight attendant laughed artificially, casting a desperate look at Sergeant Poole. He smiled and shook his head and shrugged. The sergeant seemed to know when he'd been bested.

In a reasoning-with-a-child tone, the young lady went on. "It's not *precisely* that the animal can't go in—"

Here comes some other big lie, thought James Carlton, studying the faces of the people probably waiting to board his flight and deciding which ones he wasn't going to sit beside.

". . . it's the quarantine laws. The cat would have to be quarantined for nine months, you see . . ."

"That's a pretty stupid law. This cat don't—doesn't—have rabies, nor anything like that. For the lord's sakes, I been kidnapped with this cat for five, six days. *I* ought to know. You got any *idea* what this cat's been through?"

Actually, the cat hadn't been through all that much, considering. Except for being forcibly yanked down that big tree.

The poor young woman shrugged. "I don't make the laws, James—" And then she did something utterly unthinkable, at least as far as James Carlton was concerned. She pinned a tag to his sweater and patted it.

A tag? He craned his neck to look at it. *It had*

his name and destination on it. So horrified was he that he forgot his manners, not to say his education. "Ah, hell, lady! I ain't wearing *that!* I know who I am and I know where I'm going!" He yanked the tag off and handed it back.

White-faced, she seemed truly not to know what to do. "We're merely trying to assure that you don't get—" And even as she brought out the word it was clear she'd have liked to retract it: "—lost."

Sergeant Poole burst out laughing.

When Jimmy Farraday arrived at Heathrow Airport at nine fifty-five that same night, it was difficult to say which of them—Farraday or Penny—was happier to see him.

Farraday tried on his gruff act—cigar in mouth, small punch at Jimmy's shoulder—but it soon broke down into a simple embrace. Penny's own joy was expressed in a plethora of salty words and newly handled cigarettes (the latter supplied by Jury). When Penny's enthusiasm for Scotland Yard was about to burst, Jury gave her a look.

The look silenced Penny, but it was clear that Jimmy had seen the whatever-secret-knowledge that had passed between them, and stuck out his hand. "Pleased," was his simple and heartfelt acknowledgment of this grown-up towering over him.

(Jury noticed he had quickly rid himself of

that other grown-up—the one following him in British Air uniform.)

"Pleased, myself," said Jury. And he was, for the first time in days.

James Carlton Farraday, who had left the past and all of its trials behind him for the present, turned his attention to his sister, and gave directions in the manner of one who would not be crossed.

The first was: "Watch your language, Penny. I told you, They always know by how you talk."

The second: "We got a new cat. They wouldn't let me bring it."

The third: "They had this movie on the plane I swore I seen—saw—before—"

And they were walking away, when Penny asked, "Yeah? What was it?"

"*Missing*," said Jimmy Farraday. "It was kind of dumb—"

Jury noticed that J.C. Farraday walked a respectful distance behind brother and sister, sister now taking brother's hand—

As Jimmy said, "Except it had Sissy Spacek in it." Then he seemed to look quickly around him, making sure no Memory that had been listening over the years was butting in. "Remember?"

Jury had never felt Heathrow to be so unpeopled, such a void, as he felt it now.

Penny answered, "I remember."

III

STRATFORD

"Brightness falls from the air."

—*Thomas Nashe*

36

"The computer guy," said Sam Lasko again, shaking his head in wonder. "I can't get over it. He seemed like such an elf."

Lasko and Jury were sitting in the incidents room in the Stratford police station. "One I don't want to see under any mushrooms," said Jury. "He planned it for a long time. A very long time."

"You don't seem too happy about it."

"No. Am I supposed to be?"

"I only mean, in figuring it out. I really *did* think it was some creep around here had nothing better to do with his time—"

Jury smiled. "The way you put things, Sammy . . ."

Lasko shrugged. "Well, you know what I mean. Anyway, I was sorry to see you go." Lasko's expression turned mournful, as if Jury were a too-seldom-seen relation.

"I'd never have guessed."

"So where'd Schoenberg get the passport?"

"In the U.S. One assignment he gave that private detective was to get one of Jimmy's school pictures. The little ones they do over there. Just right for a passport. And then produce a facsimile of a birth certificate, which he got very easily merely by making a request as Jimmy's father. He was really the only one, besides brother Jonathan, who knew what name was on the certificate."

"And he took that kid all the way back to the *States* . . ." Lasko sighed. "You ever been—?"

"No, Sammy. But Penny Farraday nearly had me swear on a Bible I'd come and visit them."

Lasko shook his head. "I can't get over this Schoenberg. To go to all that *trouble*—?"

"The man was obsessed, Sammy. He'd been going to a lot of trouble for *years*. Private detectives, the lot."

"Christ. The guy must have gone absolutely off the rails over this Altman woman."

"He did. 'Dust hath closed Helen's eye.'" Jury pocketed his cigarettes and stood up. "He definitely did. See you later, Sammy."

Jury was nearly out the door when Lasko (who had all the while been eying certain papers on his desk) said, "Listen, Richard—"

"Forget it, Sammy."

37

Beyond the Royal Shakespeare Theatre, the river Avon flowed on, undisturbed.

"*Hamlet* again," said Melrose Plant. "Are you sure I can't induce you to join me? The first part was quite good. I missed the second." He did not want to go into his reasons for missing the second part of the play, not once, but twice.

"Thanks, no," said Jury. "I think I've had enough of revenge tragedies to last me awhile." It was evening, and there was a storm coming on, and light had fled from the water. Jury watched the ducks bobbing in the shadows of the willows, like lumps of coal. "You're going back to Northants tomorrow?"

"Yes, I expect so. When Agatha's there, one occasionally has to count the silver. The American cousins, happily, have returned to Wisconsin. I believe they must have hightailed it out of here after the last . . . well, you know. Not even Agatha's plying them with promises of high teas at the manor house—as I'm sure she did do— could keep them here. So the Biggets and Honeysuckle Tours are all safely at home by now. I think I should like to visit Hialeah racetrack. I would imagine Lady Dew is odds-on favorite. Well, if you won't attend the theatre, then how about a drink at the Duck afterwards?"

"I have a bit of business to attend to."

"I see."

"No, you don't."

"No, I don't."

Jury smiled. "You're a very accommodating chap, you know."

"I know."

There was a brief silence, and then Jury said, "Do you really think she's going to marry that bloke?"

Innocently, Melrose inquired, " 'She'? 'Bloke'?"

Looking across the water, Jury said, "Awful, wasn't he? I shouldn't have thought Vivian would go in for that type." He glanced at Melrose. "Did you find her much changed?"

"Vivian? Vivian?" Plant stalled around by inspecting his gold cigarette case.

"At times, you can be tiresome. Yes, 'Vivian-Vivian.' Didn't you go on about the old days with her?"

Melrose plucked out a cigarette and offered the case to Jury. "Good lord, no. Barely exchanged the time of day."

Jury took a cigarette, and just looked at him, shaking his head.

"Anyway, they're not married yet. If I know Vivian, she won't go through with it. Never could make up her mind about anything important." Leaving that cloudy judgment hanging in air, Melrose looked at his watch. "I'd better be going. I'll miss the second part *again*. If you *should* change your mind, I'll be in the Dirty Duck after the play. . . ." Melrose paused a moment, and then said, "I suppose you'd as soon forget the whole business. But at one point in that business of questioning Schoenberg, you weren't exactly hell-on-wheels. You certainly left the room quickly enough, there at the end."

"Yes. Maybe it was because I didn't much care for my own reactions: I mean, I stood there knowing what Schoenberg had done, and yet—" Jury looked out over the darkening water. "He loved her that much."

38

Jury walked down Ryland Street to Number 10 and knocked on the door. A woman, small and kind-eyed, answered.

"I'm a friend of Lady Kennington. Is she in?"

The little woman looked so puzzled that for a moment Jury thought he must have come to the wrong house. But then her face cleared. "Oh, you mean Jenny, is that it?" When Jury nodded, she said, "But I'm so sorry. You see, she's gone."

There was in the word such a note of finality, Jury didn't have to question its meaning. His own face, however, must have registered such disappointment that she felt herself the author of it, a messenger come for the express purpose of bearing terrible news. "Really, I *am* sorry. It was yesterday. She moved just yesterday."

Yesterday. It had to have been yesterday.

When Jury did not reply, the messenger seemed to feel she had to make it all as clear as possible. "She got a call from a relative, I think. I believe she left sooner than she expected to." The woman apparently wanted in some small way to defend this action on the part of Lady Kennington, which might have been regarded as somewhat capricious by this stranger on her doorstep, who was not replying and still not moving. "I've only just moved in today, you see." There was a tiny, artificial laugh. "Haven't got myself sorted out yet, really."

"I'm sorry I've disturbed you—"

Her hand moved in a fluttering gesture as she said quickly, "Oh, not at all, no." There was a tentative move then, away from the door, and an invitation for Jury to enter, as if she felt she were adding insult to injury by being inhospitable as well as uninformative.

He thanked her, but shook his head. "She didn't happen to leave a message for anyone, did she?"

Sadness seemed actually to smite her, to make her feel ashamed, as she shook her head. "Not with me, she didn't. Of course, you might try the estate agent."

He thanked her again and realized, only after she had closed the door, he hadn't got the name of the estate agent from her. He raised his hand to knock again and then let it fall. Tomorrow—

Walking back up the street he wondered if he would return tomorrow or if fate had decided the matter for him.

Jury crossed the street between the Dirty Duck and the theatre, walking toward the river, aimlessly. Under the branches of the line of oaks, each tree decorated with strings of lights, as if it were Christmas, came the last of the theatregoers, their umbrellas black against the reflected light, runners in the rain, late for the performance.

He sat on the same bench near the river where he had sat with Penny what seemed an age ago, his hands bunched in his coat pockets, unmindful of the rain. When it was full dark, he got up and walked back toward the theatre, the parking lot attendant leaning bored against his kiosk, as behind the glass doors of the theatre the black-uniformed ushers looked out, apparently equally bored. Jury took the path that ran in total darkness behind the theatre and near the river, and that passed the brass-rubbing center.

It was from that direction he heard the drowsy laughter that sharpened at his approach into giggles, although he knew they couldn't see him in this pitch-darkness. Schoolchildren—he knew it from the giggles and the lighted coals of cigarettes. When he was closer he could make out the boys sitting on the wall of the Doric-columned building. It wasn't until he was nearly on top of them that they saw him. The laughter stopped quickly, and the voices.

They were out here larking when they probably were supposed to be inside, watching Shakespeare and getting educated.

Some giggles again, and whispers when they realized someone was out here on the walk. As matches spurted and cigarettes were being lit up in acts of bravado, one of them asked; "Who's there?"

Jury peered into the darkness of the colon-naded building, unable to see anyone or any-thing except the butt ends of the cigarettes. He could make out the school uniforms of the ones who had been sitting (but who had hopped up when they saw him). They were all dressed alike, the ones he could see. As a few more came out of the darkness—curiosity having finally out-weighed the fear of getting caught—he made out six or seven, a few others still stopping back there in the safer dark, and still giggling nervously.

In a tone that one of the boys probably re-garded as a display of fearlessness in the face of authority, the question was repeated: "Well, who's *there?*"

"Nobody," said Jury. Tiny flames spurted and they began to light up cigarettes again.

"You're not a *teacher* or anything, are you?" came a voice out of the darkness, suspicious.

"Good lord, no."

There was a mutual, silent turning-over of this answer. "What are you *doing* out here?"

"Taking a walk." He smiled into the darkness. "What are *you* doing out here in the brass-rubbing center?"

More giggles and a small-girl voice from the darkness replied, "There's more'n brass gets rubbed out here." From the fresh giggles, Jury imagined there was a good deal of clumsy groping going on.

"Tell us who you are, then," said a girl who Jury estimated was a year or two younger than Penny. She had stepped forth as if separating herself from her mates, who were a bit silly, when she meant business.

"Nobody. I told you."

For some reason, she now felt it necessary to jump from the edge of the structure down to the ground and walk heavily about, trampling down the black loam where, probably, a gardener had been hard at work planting. "That's what Odysseus said."

"It is?"

"Well, you've *heard* of Odysseus, I expect." Her tone was condescending and also announced that if she was neglecting Shakespeare tonight, she was not neglecting the Greeks. "You know. When he was in the Cyclops' cave. It's how he got away, saying he was Nobody."

"Maybe that's what he meant. Or Homer did."

Jury's reward for this unwanted insight was a giant sigh, as the girl tramped heavily about in this newly-budded garden and then hitched herself back up and onto the edge of the building. He could make out little of her face, except to see it was ghostly-white and heart-shaped and fringed by long hair.

He continued on his way, along the unlit path, uncertain of where it led. They would be glad to be rid of him, another adult intruding on their few stolen moments of privacy.

But when he'd got perhaps a hundred feet away he heard the voice of the girl call good-bye in a tone which rather surprised him, the tone of one who shared a secret.

Jury turned and made them a salute and called good-bye. All he saw then in the total dark was the coal-end of one cigarette as its owner inhaled before flicking it away. It made a small arc of light, and then dimmed and went out, its brightness falling from air.

DON'T MISS MARTHA GRIMES'S
OTHER DAZZLING RICHARD JURY
MYSTERIES . . .

The Man with a Load of Mischief

*Introducing Scotland Yard's Richard Jury in
Martha Grimes's intriguing first novel*

At the Man with a Load of Mischief, a dead man is
found with his head stuck in a beer keg. At the Jack
and Hammer, another body was stuck out on the beam
of the pub's sign, replacing the mechanical man who
kept the time. Two pubs. Two murders. One Scotland
Yard inspector called in to help. Detective Chief Inspector Richard Jury arrives in Long Piddleton and
finds everyone in the postcard village looking outside
of town for the killer. Except for Melrose Plant. A keen
observer of human nature, he points Jury in the right
direction: toward the darkest parts of his neighbors'
hearts. . . .

"Grimes captures the flavor of British village life. . . .
Long may she write Richard Jury mysteries."
—*Chicago Tribune*

The Old Fox Deceiv'd

Stacked against the cliffs on the shore of the North Sea and nearly hidden by fog, the town of Rackmoor seems a fitting place for murder. But the stabbing death of a costumed young woman has shocked the close-knit village. When Richard Jury arrives on the scene, he's pulled up short by the fact that no one is sure who the victim is, much less the killer. Her questionable ties to one of the most wealthy and influential families in town send Jury and Melrose Plant on a deadly hunt to track down a very wily murderer.

"A superior writer."

—*The New York Times Book Review*

"Warmth, humor, and great style . . . a thoroughly satisfying plot . . . one of the smoothest, richest traditional English mysteries ever to originate on this side of the Atlantic." —*Kirkus Reviews*

I Am the Only Running Footman

They were two women, strikingly similar in life . . . strikingly similar in death. Both were strangled with their own scarves—one in Devon, one outside a fashionable Mayfair pub called I Am the Only Running Footman. Richard Jury teams up with Devon's irascible local divisional commander, Brian Macalvie, to solve the murders. With nothing to tie the women together but the fatal scarves, Jury pursues his only suspect . . . and a trail of tragedy that just might lead to yet another victim—and her killer.

"Everything about Miss Grimes's new novel shows her at her best. . . . [She] gets our immediate attention. . . . She holds it, however, with something more than mere suspense." —*The New Yorker*

"Literate, witty, and stylishly crafted." —*The Washington Post*

The Five Bells and Bladebone

Richard Jury has yet to finish his first pint in the village of Long Piddleton when he finds a corpse inside a beautiful rosewood desk recently acquired by the local antiques dealer, Marshall Trueblood. The body belongs to Simon Lean, a notorious philanderer. An endless list of suspects leads Jury and his aristocratic sidekick, Melrose Plant, to the nearby country estate where Lean's long-suffering wife resides. But Jury's best clue comes in London at a pub called the Five Bells and Bladebone. There he learns about Lean's liaison with a disreputable woman named Sadie, who could have helped solve the case . . . if she wasn't already dead.

"Blends almost Dickensian sketches of character and social class with glimpses of a ferocious marriage."
—*Time*

"[Grimes's] best . . . as moving as it is entertaining."
—*USA Today*

The Case Has Altered

Timeless, peaceful, and remote, the watery Lincolnshire fens seem an unlikely setting for murder. But two women—a notorious actress and a servant girl—have been killed there in the space of two weeks. The Lincolnshire police are sure the murders are connected—and they think a friend of Richard Jury is responsible. Jury is anxious to clear Jenny Kennington's name. But the secretive suspects and tight-lipped locals are leading him nowhere. And with the help of his colleague Melrose Plant, he must struggle to navigate a series of untruths in the hope of stopping a very determined killer.

"Masterful writing, skillful plotting, shrewd characterizations, subtle humor, and an illuminating look at what makes us humans tick . . . [an] outstanding story from one of today's most talented writers . . . brilliant."

—*Booklist*

"Dazzling. Deftly plotted . . . psychologically complex . . . delicious wit."   —*Publishers Weekly*

The Stargazey

After a luminous blonde leaves, reboards, then leaves the double-decker bus Richard Jury is on, he follows her up to the gates of Fulham Palace . . . and goes no farther. Days later, when he hears of the death in the palace's walled garden, Jury will wonder if he could have averted it. But is the victim the same woman Jury saw? As he and Melrose Plant follow the complex case from the Crippsian depths of London's East End to the headier heights of Mayfair's art scene, Jury will realize that in this captivating woman—dead or alive—he may have finally met his match. . . .

"A delightfully entertaining blend of irony, danger, and intrigue, liberally laced with wit and charm. . . . A must have from one of today's most gifted and intelligent writers."   —*Booklist* (starred review)

"The literary equivalent of a box of Godiva truffles . . . wonderful."   —*Los Angeles Times*

The Lamorna Wink

With his good friend Richard Jury on a fool's errand in Northern Ireland, Melrose Plant tries—in vain—to escape his aunt and his Long Piddleton lethargy by fleeing to Cornwall. There, high on a rocky promontory overlooking the sea, he rents a house—one furnished with tragic memories. But his Cornwallian reveries are tempered by the local waiter/cab driver/amateur magician. The industrious Johnny Wells seems unflappable—until his beloved aunt disappears. Now Plant is dragged into the disturbing pasts of everyone involved—and a murder mystery that only Richard Jury can solve. ....

"Swift and satisfying . . . grafts the old-fashioned 'Golden Age' amateur-detective story to the contemporary police procedural . . . real charm."
—*The Wall Street Journal*

"Entrancing. Grimes makes her own mark on du Maurier country." —*The Orlando Sentinel*

The Blue Last

Mickey Haggerty, a DCI with the City police, has asked for Richard Jury's help. Two skeletons have been unearthed during the excavation of London's last bomb site, where once stood a pub called the Blue Last. The grandchild of brewery magnate Oliver Tynedale supposedly survived that December 1940 bombing . . . but did she? Then the son of the onetime owner of the Blue Last is found shot to death—the book he was writing about London during the German blitzkrieg . . . gone. A stolen life, a stolen book? Or is any of this what it seems? With Melrose Plant sent undercover, Jury calls into question identity, memory, and provenance in a case that resurrects his own hauntingly sad past. . . .

"Grimes's best . . . a cliffhanger ending."

—*USA Today*

"Explosive . . . ranks among the best of its creator's distinguished work."　　　—*Richmond Times-Dispatch*